CAPTURED

LOLA
TAYLOR

Rogue werewolf Elijah Johnson would have been better off dead. After being held hostage by a coven of malicious witches—witches who seem to know much more about the dark arts than they should—he takes the first chance he can to escape, only to fall into a trap a month later. When he's captured during a DPI bust, he expects to be thrown into prison. He doesn't expect to learn his interrogator is a curvy young witch with hair the color of fire and enough passion for the law to match...

Verika Tate has spent her career trying to uphold the values and morals of law enforcement in the Underworld. Only twenty-six, she is heralded as one of the most gifted witches in the southeastern region. Her life is, for the most part, uneventful. She attends her weekly spellbook club meetings, works out daily to try to shed some stubborn fat that refuses to leave, and buries her nose in the latest witchcraft magazines. Learning is her shield and her only defense for being able to forget the werewolf who broke her heart—Nik Johnson...

When she's assigned to Elijah, she can hardly believe how rotten her luck is. He looks enough like Nik to haunt her, and his hard muscle and flirtatious quips are enough to make her pant. Verika struggles to keep her heart out of her work, a point which proves especially tricky when Elijah reveals an astonishing secret that could finally break the case she's been trying to crack—the whereabouts of the mysterious Mistress Black, leader of the witch mafia. The tip is too good to pass up, and she reluctantly agrees to help him escape the witches who have placed a bounty on his head in exchange for information.

Will Verika uphold the law at any cost, or will she risk everything for the sake of a once-in-a-lifetime romance?

Cover designed by Kitten of Deranged Doctor Design
Interior design and formatting by Champagne Formats
Editing by Jen of Mistress Editing
Indigo Dreamer Press logo designed by Indi99o of 99designs
Author photograph by Sara Rogers Photography

www.lolataylorbooks.com
www.indigodreamerpress.com

INDIGO
DREAMER PRESS

ISBN-10: 0-9981140-1-4
ISBN-13: 978-0-9981140-1-9

For more information, please visit
www.lolataylorbooks.com

CHAPTER ONE

ELIJAH JOHNSON STUMBLED IN THE DARKNESS. FOR ALL his grace as a werewolf, he was clumsy as an injured human.

More like a drugged human.

The potion he'd drunk to break the Tracking spell on him was strong. It laced his veins with venom, making him delirious as he ran. He would have preferred to run on four paws, but one of the side effects of the potion was that it muted his ability to change.

Fine by him. No price was too high if it meant escaping this hell on earth.

He didn't dare look back at the mansion behind him, though he could feel it watching him, like a sentient being.

Damn those witches.

The place gave him the damn creeps. Not for the first time, he inwardly kicked himself for being so reckless and getting drawn into their fucked-up world.

Not that he had anything against witches. That is, he *didn't have* a grudge before all this shit straight out of a horror movie happened.

Now… he'd never go near another damn witch again.

Run. Run faster.

The woods seemed to be closing in on him, but that was probably just his paranoia. At least, he thought it was until a tree root lifted of its own accord and tripped him. He swore, swinging his arms out to right his balance.

A groan, followed by splintering wood, came from beside him. He looked up to see the tree bending over.

Shit like this shouldn't have surprised him. God knows he'd seen enough weird things in the Order to make most sane people lose their minds.

But seeing a tree falling toward him, to watch its bark twist and snap as it fought to angle itself just right, still made him pause.

Snap out of it, dipshit!

Shaking his head, he blinked and leapt out of the way at the last second. The tree came crashing down, making the ground shudder.

Dammit, if they hadn't realized he'd escaped before, they sure as hell would now. He needed to haul ass out of here, pronto.

Scrambling to his feet, he struggled up the hill as the air filled with the rustle of thousands of leaves and the groan of snapping wood.

He caught movement from the corners of his eyes, and he glanced around him.

His eyes widened. *Shit.*

The whole damned forest was *coming to life*.

Moonlight shone through the trees, dappling the forest floor with patches of silver light. It danced and shifted as the trees uprooted themselves and began to stalk toward him. Even the bushes rustled and chittered like angry dogs.

Damn!

He knew there was a spell around the perimeter to keep him from leaving. He thought he'd broken it, along with the other five back-up spells they'd cast. He had not detected this.

Those bitches had sent a tree army after him.

He growled and tried going faster, but it was all he could do to keep up the pace he was going. The potion made him slow. He hadn't counted on it being this bad. In order to keep them from catching on, he couldn't afford to test the potion before using it.

Another reckless risk on his part, in a long list of many.

He squinted. Just ahead, up on a hill, sat the dirt path leading to the enchanted mansion. Seeing that road filled him with renewed hope, spurring him to run faster. His heels dug into the earth, swiftly finding purchase on the soil as he scurried toward the path to freedom.

Not far now...

He was going to make it.

A whip-like vine shot out of the darkness, lassoing his neck. It jerked backward, tugging him back toward the woods. With a yelp, he lost his footing and fell over a log that had positioned itself to trip him.

So help him God, he was going to set this whole place on fire if he ever did escape.

The hill flew past his line of vision in a blur of moss, weeds, and moonlight. The breath left him as his back slammed against the ground. The back of his head banged against a rock, making him see stars for a few seconds. Sharp pain shot through the back of his skull, and he bit down on his lip to keep from crying out.

Vines tangled around his limbs as he struggled to get up. He snarled and fought, reaching inside himself to try to summon his inner wolf, but it wouldn't come.

He was alone.

The ground began to sink around him. Feeling fresh, damp soil pouring onto his body, his terror spiked and he fought like a man possessed.

Apparently, the plants had decided it would be a good idea to bury him alive. More like, *the witches* had decided to bury him alive.

This was just like Black to pull this twisted shit. She was probably watching him right now in a crystal ball or something, laughing her ass off.

At one point in his life, he might have found it funny, too. A practical joke. He had been a very different man a year ago, had done a lot of shit he regretted, things that kept him up at night.

He never should have come here. Now, it looked like he was never going to leave.

As he sank deeper into the earth, surrounded by darkness, a seductive voice whispered a message inside his head.

"I told you, Elijah. We're meant to be together. You'll never be able to escape me."

"Damn… you…" he got out, right before the earth collapsed on top of him completely and all went pitch-black.

CHAPTER TWO

"H EY, WAKE UP, BUB! GET OUT! WE'RE HERE."

"Huh?" Elijah's head lolled forward. His chin smacked against his chest, driving his teeth into his tongue. He winced as blood filled his mouth. His head felt like it was full of goop. Son of a bitch, was he groggy. That damned potion had done a number on him.

A hand grabbed his arm and tugged. "Didn't you hear me, pot head? I said get the hell out of my truck."

"Jesus, all right," Elijah said, waving the irritable truck driver off. "I'm moving."

Though he was still dizzy as hell, he managed to clamber out of the truck and grab his duffel bag. He looked like shit. The bill on his ball cap was crooked, and the Velcro adjustment on the back had been torn off. It, more or less, just lay on his head. Dirt covered his stolen jeans and the soles were coming undone on his boots, which were about a size too small. His dingy navy blue T-shirt had definitely

6

seen better days. He didn't think the holes in it were of the fashionable kind.

The truck driver raised his brows and crossed his arms. "Well? You gonna pay?"

Elijah had enough sense left to look around. "This is the middle of nowhere. I told you to take me to Destiny."

"We are in Destiny, the city limits anyway." He turned pointed behind them, to some lights Elijah could barely make out in the distance. "It's about twenty miles or so down that way. If you hurry, you can be there before dawn."

Elijah's teeth ground together. "I said take me to Destiny, not twenty miles outside of Destiny."

"I said I'd get you as close as I could." He glanced around, as if expecting someone to pop out of the sprawling, grassy plains around them. "Word over the radio has it the DPI has been crawling over that place for the past week. Don't know what they're looking for, but I can't afford to get caught."

"Yeah," Elijah said dryly, glancing at the back of the semi in the cargo bay. "All those crates of illegal potions might not go over too well with them."

That spooked the man. "Just pay me my money so I can be on my way, asshole."

Elijah growled low in his throat, his eyes flashing gold. He could tear into this man and leave him here for dead. A year ago, he might have. But he wasn't that man anymore. He'd stopped batting for Team Evil a long time ago, as soon as its charm wore off.

Elijah reached into his back pocket for his billfold and

produced a hundred-dollar bill. "Here you go."

The man took it and frowned. "I said two hundred."

"You said no such thing. And if you try to scam me, I may have to reconsider punching in what teeth you have left."

Fear flashed through the man's eyes for a second. Spitting on the ground, he stalked toward his cab with a scowl. "Damn werewolves," he muttered. "Can't trust any of 'em."

Elijah smiled grimly. *You got that right.*

As the man got in and drove off, Elijah hitched his bag over his shoulder and began walking.

He could feel blisters rubbing on the heels of his feet. This was going to suck.

Different topics went through his head, but his thoughts were mostly preoccupied with what the hell he was going to do with his life. The "buried alive" dream kept replaying over and over in his head. He hadn't actually been buried alive, or at least, he didn't think he had. Someone had found him shivering and naked by the highway and had taken him to a hospital. Once he realized where he was, he'd stolen some clothing and scrammed before they could figure out his identity. He wouldn't put it past Black to have spies everywhere.

He shuddered just thinking about her.

Could he really get away from her? Had it all just been a childish fantasy?

Anger at all the things she'd made him do—all the things he'd somewhat enjoyed doing, before his wake-up call—rekindled his determination.

He would change his name. Move to Europe. Hell, move to Antarctica if that's what it took.

All he knew was he could never go back there. He'd rather die than succumb to that kind of darkness again.

He took a moment to take in a deep breath of chilly air and survey his surroundings. Tennessee countryside really was beautiful. He hadn't spent much time here except in passing, but he'd always admired the lush grass and plentiful trees. Yes, he still loved to look at trees in autumn bloom, even after they'd tried to kill him. He sympathized with them, in a way. They were as much Black's puppets as he had been.

In the back of his mind loomed his brothers' faces. They were never far from his thoughts. Neither was the guilt at leaving them, or the yearning to see them again.

His fingers itched to call them, but he never did. He couldn't afford to have them dragged into his mess. There would never come a day when he would ever place them in danger.

It has to be this way, for their own good.

He lost track of time as he walked. Twenty miles really wasn't that long when you had plenty on your mind.

The city of Destiny wasn't very big, about twenty thousand people, more or less, according to Google.

Being nearly dawn, the city was just awakening. Wanting to draw the least amount of attention to himself as possible, he cut a path through the woods, well away from the highway.

There weren't that many pedestrians out yet, though his inner sense of the supernatural picked up on a few signatures. It wasn't unusual for vampires to be out this late, though they would retire soon. Paranormal creatures in general were more active at night.

The twinkling stars overhead were beginning to fade away as the sky lightened. He glanced at his watch. It was nearly six a.m. His contact would be waiting for him.

He had arranged transportation weeks ago in the black market, as well as a fake passport and other identification, with another werewolf who went by Shade. Shade was an astute businessman, with a knack for staying off the DPI's radar. Granted, had Elijah known the DPI was staking out this city for some reason, he might not have been so keen to meet Shade here.

Oh, well. It couldn't be helped. Ever since rumors had begun to circulate about a witch mafia killing off paranormals, the DPI had doubled its police efforts. Stakeouts like these were more common now. He knew he'd have to be careful before he'd even made the decision to escape.

He just hoped all that planning wasn't about to be blown sky-high.

Elijah was walking by a pay phone when it began to ring.

He stopped.

Shit like that was too coincidental. And his gut was hardly ever wrong. Sensing it was for him, he walked over to it and answered. He waited, not wanting to be the first to speak.

"Is this the traveler?" came a gravelly voice from the other side amid a sheen of static.

Elijah tensed. Shade always did have a very distinctive

voice. "Yeah."

"Your roommate came home early," Shade went on.

Elijah frowned. "The roommate" had to be the DPI.

Damn. How had they found him? Shade was infamous for evading them. *It would be this one time…* "That's too bad."

"Tell me about it. Location's changed. Go to location B."

The line went dead and Elijah hung up the phone. He'd heard the regret in Shade's voice. For a crook, Shade really was an honest one, at least to his business associates. He would never intentionally throw somebody under the bus. Not many "honest" people could say as much.

Elijah deliberated.

If he had any sense, he'd tuck tail and put as much distance between him and the DPI as possible. And he would have, had he any other trustworthy contacts. The IDs and all his false paperwork—the tickets to his freedom and a new life, away from the Order—were only another block away. Another chance like this might not crop up for a long time, and then he'd be trapped in the States for a while.

Trapped in the same country as Mistress Black.

Chills broke out over his skin as a shudder rolled through him. He'd never relive the horrors she'd put him through again, so help him God.

He took off walking, following the street signs until he got to the right place.

The diner was modest and plain, the type of place that didn't draw too much attention to itself.

And the perfect place for a back-up meeting.

Scanning every which way for potential DPI agents, Elijah donned his sunglasses and casually entered the diner.

The lights were dim and eighties rock played from an old jukebox in the corner. Guests were eating breakfast, making idle chit-chat. There was so much smoke in the air it was a bit hazy.

Elijah saw Shade sitting in a shadowy booth in a corner. He was wearing a black cowboy hat and a black leather jacket that seemed to blend in with the shadows.

Elijah walked over to him and ordered a coffee from the waitress.

Shade looked up, his gray eyes piercing. "Were you followed?"

"Don't think so."

"You don't think or you don't know?"

Elijah stared at him evenly. "I don't know," he admitted.

With a grunt, Shade slid a manila envelope over to Elijah, who discreetly slid him an envelope full of cash.

Shade stood quickly and tipped his hat. "Pleasure doing business with you."

He started out the door when the front door opened and in walked a man and a woman wearing matching uniforms.

Elijah felt Shade's fear before he read the initials stitched with golden thread on the couple's jackets.

DPI.

Stay. Calm.

Shade pretended like he dropped something and

then chuckled. He pointed toward the rear. "Forgot I was parked out back," he mumbled, without looking at Elijah.

Elijah knew the man was trying to keep from incriminating him, which he appreciated.

Too bad it didn't work.

Down the hall, he heard a door open and startled cries from the kitchen staff as a herd of footsteps thundered toward the dining room.

Shade swore and whirled, but the agents were quicker.

Elijah froze, surveying the situation.

His werewolf ears picked up more doors bursting open throughout the building. Agents clad in the token midnight blue uniform of the DPI SWAT team raided the room, their guns raised. He knew they didn't need them. They were mostly for show more than anything, a "last resort," in case their spells failed. Most of the DPI was comprised of the most talented witches and warlocks on the planet, since magic usually trumped fangs or fur in any fight.

"You have got to be kidding me."

All these months of painstakingly planning every move, and he had walked right into a bust.

An agent stopped in front of him and raised her weapon. Everyone in the room froze as the DPI surrounded him and Shade.

The woman's eyes flicked to his shoulder. "Drop the bag and raise your hands, now!"

No problem. He didn't need the bag. There wasn't anything in there of much use, anyway, and definitely nothing that could incriminate him.

Frantic, he wracked his brain for options. He could try to run, but he'd be gunned down quickly. And all his exits were blocked.

Gritting his teeth, he slowly held up his hands.

"Fine. I surrender."

CHAPTER THREE

HOLY SHIT. SHE WAS GOING TO DIE.

Verika's heart pounded as the treadmill beeped, signaling her last lap.

She'd been running every morning for the past week, and she still felt as out-of-breath now as she did on day one. And yet, she relished the breathlessness and the sweat. She always felt more relaxed after a run. Maybe what people said was true—exercise really did help stress.

And boy, could she use some help in that department.

Ever since the witch mafia started its killing spree, all agents had been working around the clock to stop them. Verika didn't mind being busy—and hey, all the overtime fattened up her paychecks—but she was sick of the investigation not going anywhere.

Where the hell were these witches and warlocks? Why hadn't they been able to find them yet?

Being a bit of a spellbook-worm, Verika had always

fancied herself adept at Tracking spells. Whenever there was a tough case to crack, they called her to locate a criminal in hiding or find a loophole in a spell. And she always did.

Until now.

Whomever the Order was employing, they were very good. And in her world, "very good" probably meant the witch in question obtained such a powerful spell by illegal means.

Her stomach rolled at the thought of some of the dark spells she'd come across in her hours and hours of research and study. Blood magic was so unpredictable that few people were allowed to practice it, and even then, you had to be licensed and registered with the Department of Magical Affairs. Every practicing witch had to register, and each type of magic had a fee associated with it. The more dangerous the magic, the higher the license and registration fees, not to mention the tests you had to take… After all was said and done, the whole deal could be astronomically pricey.

Thus, not many witches or warlocks were actually licensed to practice Blood Magic. Verika thought it would be a breeze to find the ring leader of the Order—the mysterious Mistress Black—but so far, all of their leads had run cold. She'd come across so many dead ends that she was starting to feel like she was getting nowhere.

The treadmill beeped, and Verika slammed her palm down on the stop button with a huge sigh. She slowed to a walk as the track came to a stop. Gripping the rails, she bent over and panted, trying to catch her breath. Her stomach growled and she looked down. "Easy there," she murmured hoarsely, taking a towel and wiping the sweat from her brow and chest. "I'll get you something to eat."

Stepping off the treadmill, which was in her office/study, she walked down the hall of her apartment and into the kitchen. Her scale gleamed up at her from its spot on the floor beside her fridge. She thought it would be a good deterrent to snacking on things that wouldn't help her love handles disappear. Or the extra flab on her arms, or her thunder thighs, or her—

Gah! Stop thinking about your figure!

She opened the fridge and stared at its contents. Water, non-sweet tea, fresh fruit slices, salad, salad, more salad, dark chocolate…

Her mouth watered as she gazed longingly at the chocolate. The scale seemed to taunt her. "How many calories does that have?" it seemed to say.

"But it's dark chocolate!" her conscience wanted to argue. "It's the good-for-you chocolate."

She could just imagine the scale's disapproving stare.

With a big sigh, she grabbed a bag of peach slices and some water before shutting the fridge. She set it down on the counter, and while fishing through her silverware drawer, her cell phone went off.

Though it was nearly dawn, it didn't surprise her. HQ was always calling her at odd hours: in the middle of the night, on Christmas Eve, on her birthday of all days… There were never truly any days off when you were a field agent.

Verika didn't even bother glancing at the ID as she

answered the phone. "The Imperial March" ring tone was enough of a giveaway as to who was calling. "Tate," she said.

"We need you to come down."

"What's the occasion?" she asked, already rounding the countertop and heading to the bathroom to shower.

"We got a new suspect in the witch mafia case."

Her heart started to beat faster. Despite all the setbacks, she still hoped for a breakthrough, for a lead that would finally shed some light on this abysmal case. "I'm listening."

"I'm emailing you his file right now. We don't have much on him. He has some pretty powerful identity spells around him that I need you to crack first."

Interesting. "I'll be there in twenty."

She flipped her phone closed and turned on the hot water. After a quick shower, she applied some light makeup, coupled her favorite pair of pants with some ankle-high, flat black boots and a pretty, black, short-sleeved sweater, and put some silver hoops into her ears. She grabbed her fruit and water and headed out the door.

Traffic was starting to pick up as the sun's first rays broke the horizon, scattering orange light everywhere. Weaving through the interstate exits, she quickly made it to the main headquarters in downtown Foxboro, Tennessee.

The nice thing about Foxboro was that it was just big enough to feel like a city, but not so big that you felt like you were going to be swallowed up by it. Parts of it still reminded her of the small, Southern town she'd grown up in, back in Florida.

She used a text-to-voice app on her phone to have the suspect's profile read to her on the way over. Her boss was right; there wasn't much to go on. "John Smith, Caucasian male, werewolf, Age: unknown, Height: six foot five inches, Weight: Two-hundred and ten pounds, Eye color: blue, Hair color: black. No records could be found."

Somebody had gone to a lot of trouble to cloak him, and at great expense. Cloaking spells were also illegal and could only be used by the authorities.

The red brick building that housed the DPI's headquarters stood at the other end of the parking lot. An American flag waved in the breeze out front, right beside the flags that represented every supernatural race. It always made her proud to see those flags, to know she was helping out in her community. Back where she was from, no one really gave a damn about anyone else. It was a rotten feeling, and she'd thought the whole world was like that until she joined the agency.

Her boss met her at the door. "Our perp's downstairs in one of the de-spelling rooms," he said as they made for the elevator.

"That's okay," she said, changing directions and heading for the stairs. "I need the exercise. What room is he in?"

"Four," he said, shaking his head with a wry smile. "You and your healthy ways are starting to make me feel bad about my gut."

"It's never too late to start trying to live healthier," she said with a wink and took off for the stairs.

Excitement crept into her veins as she went down to

the next level. *Please let this guy know something.*

There were two levels below the main floor that housed all the administrative offices. One level was their laboratories and archives. The other was for all the rooms they used for interrogations and de-spellings.

Verika had a skip to her step as she cleared the stairwell and walked down the indigo-carpeted hallway to the de-spelling area. The building was decorated in much the same fashion on every floor: indigo carpet, cream-colored walls, and fluorescent lighting. The main staff all wore khakis and indigo tops while the lab techs walked around in long white lab coats. Field agents were always dressed in casual attire, in case an assignment popped up. Most wore their silver and gold badges on lanyards or clipped to their belts or jackets.

Verika wore hers on her belt. It shone in the light as she rounded the corner and spotted room four. She could make out the lone figure of a man hunched over the table. His hands were clasped and he had his forehead pressed to them. His eyes were closed, as if he was deep in thought.

From this angle, it was hard to get a good look at him, but she appreciated what she saw. The strong round of his shoulders suggested muscle underneath, and his sleeves had been rolled up to the elbow, exposing tanned, muscled skin.

She might have found his physique attractive had he not been brought in on suspicion of ties to the witch mafia. She didn't have to ask why he'd been tied to the witch mafia. She could already tell, by the signatures they gave off, that the spells on him hadn't come cheap and that they would have taken more than one witch to perform.

It definitely sounded like the work of a coven. And so far, the only coven that had been able to afford the priciest spells they'd come across was this enigmatic witch mafia.

A big sigh made his shoulders heave as she stopped outside the door and watched him through the glass. It was one-way; she could see him, but he couldn't see her.

Eager to get the ball rolling, she cleared her throat and strode into the room. "Good morning, Mr. Smith. My name's—"

The blood drained from her face as he looked up, and she abruptly drew to a halt.

Those eyes, the set of his mouth… even his face.

Nik?

CHAPTER FOUR

Elijah blinked. "Me?"

The woman continued to stare at him.

Damn. He knew he looked a little ragged, but come on, did he look that bad?

Or maybe…

A devilish grin slowly spread across his face. "What's the matter, Red? You like what you see?"

That got her attention. Her jaw promptly snapped shut, and she shook her head. When she looked at him, the shock had drained from her face, replaced by cool indifference. "Hardly." She sauntered toward him, though she looked stiff. Her movements were jerky and her jaw never quite unclenched.

He studied her as she sat across from him and crossed her legs before digging through what he presumed to be his file.

There was little in there. They wouldn't get much on

him. The Order had ensured that.

His eyes roved over the curve of the woman's jaw and the slight pout of her red lips. Beautiful vibrant red curls hung around her face. Her skin was the fairest he had seen in a while; it was pure white, with a faint dusting of sandy-colored freckles across her cheeks and arms. In a word, she was lovely. He found he couldn't take his eyes off her.

Someone rolled a cart by the door, banging it on the wall, and she jumped. She closed her eyes and pinched the bridge of her nose before resuming her frantic shuffling. If he didn't know better, he'd think she was intentionally stalling to avoid looking at him.

"You look spooked," he commented.

"You just remind me of someone I used to know," she said quickly, finally glancing up at him. The steely glare in her green eyes made it clear he should keep his mouth shut. "Mr. Smith, I'm—"

"Verika Tate."

She froze, her eyes widening. "What?"

He pointed to her hips. "I read it on your badge when you walked in. What?" He grinned. "Did you get excited?"

She pursed her lips, not replying. The hardness in her eyes began to simmer with anger. "Pissed off" was a good look on her. It only made her more beautiful.

Something stirred within him, some emotion long forgotten.

Desire.

Snap out of it, you idiot. She's a damned witch. You can't ever forget what they've done to you.

"Let's get straight to the point," Verika said, her strong

voice reverberating throughout the room. "There are some rather sophisticated cloaking spells on you, and they've called me in here to break them. Now, as you may or may not know, cloaking spells can be very… *tricky* to break. Painful, even." She smiled with fake sweetness. "And we wouldn't want any harm to come to you now, would we?"

He raised a brow, amused. And turned on. "Are you threatening me?"

"Stating facts isn't the same as threatening someone," Verika said plainly. "It's just how these things go."

"So, you must be pretty good if they called someone like you in when their supposed 'experts,'" he said with air quotes, "couldn't break the cloaking spells."

Her eyes glittered with pride. "Something like that."

He shifted his weight in the cool metal seat and propped his handcuffed hands on the chair's arms. Leveling a challenging smirk at her, he said, "Give me your best shot, Red."

She blinked a few times as color rushed to her face before clearing her throat and standing.

God, why was he still flirting with her? What the hell was his deal? She was a W.I.T.C.H. And from the looks of it a pretty powerful one at that.

Apparently, he was a masochist, because he found the need to hear that dark, sultry voice of hers was more important than listening to his common sense. Her voice had a slight southern twang to it that her coworkers lacked. She must not be from around here. He found it incredibly alluring, like a sweet-and-sultry southern belle.

She walked over to him, though she kept a few safe

inches away.

"I won't bite, Red," he said. *Though I would like to do a few other things.* He gave her a suggestive look that nearly made her face match her hair color.

"I n-need you to take your shirt off," she mumbled in a rush.

His heart skipped a beat. "Couldn't wait to get me naked, huh, sweetheart?"

"Just do it!" she snapped, looking flustered.

Verika promptly whirled and went over to a cabinet. She began taking out different sized vials of liquid. The sight of the potions sent a shiver of dread down his spine.

She gathered what she needed and turned around, pausing. "Is something wrong?"

"Nothing," he murmured, his throat suddenly feeling tighter. He instinctively started to reach for his shirt hem, until the handcuffs clanked against the arms of the chair. "A little help here?"

She blinked. "Duh," she murmured, looking surprised that she'd asked him to undress when he clearly could not. He had a feeling she was normally one of those carefully put-together girls. And the fact he was the one unraveling her composure only made his cock throb with longing.

Get. A. Grip.

She stared at his hands and muttered an incantation that sent his heart into his throat. Dammit, those witches had scarred him for life. He'd probably never be able to hear another spell again without getting a little nervous.

Verika snapped her fingers. The cuffs instantly unlocked. She removed them and tossed them onto the metal table.

He raised his brows in question.

"Go ahead," she said with a smirk, placing her hands on her curvy hips. "Try to move."

He tried raising his arms and couldn't. His pulse kicked up a notch as cold fear washed over him. "What did you do to me?"

"Relax. It's just a simple binding spell. Now arms up."

Not of his own doing, his arms shot into the air. His breath caught as terror seized him. He squeezed his eyes shut, swallowing hard. Behind his closed eyes, he saw a dark room. In the center, he dangled by cuffs from the ceiling, beneath a single blood-red light. Out of the darkness came a pair of long, tanned legs, along with a glittering black dress. The woman's scarlet lips came into the light and she smiled. "You shouldn't try to run away from your master, little pup. Didn't I tell you I owned you?"

She raised her palm and a dagger materialized in her hand. She slowly unsheathed it and ran her tongue along the blunt side of the blade, her cruel, ebony eyes fixed on him. "You've been a bad dog."

She raised the dagger—

"Mr. Smith?"

He jumped, blinking several times. His wild eyes darted about, trying to get a rein on his bearings.

The worried face of the beautiful red-haired witch gazed at him. "Dear God, you're sweating. And you're clammy. Are you okay?" She grabbed a rag and pressed it against his forehead and bare chest. She must have removed his shirt while he'd been locked in the memory.

"Just…" He swallowed hard, trying to get a grip on his breathing and hammering heart. "Just let my arms down."

Her brows stooped in confusion, but she snapped her fingers and his hands dropped back to the chair. He sagged forward, taking deep breaths and trying to clear his mind.

She slowly knelt in front of him, silent for a few breaths. "Mind telling me what that was all about?"

His throat closed up. Mutely, he shook his head. He'd avoided magic ever since he'd escaped the Order. Though he still had nightmares, and sure, he was a little jumpy, he hadn't suspected the Order had affected him like this.

He was seriously fucked up. And this witch, no matter how desirable, was not helping.

Verika didn't press him for answers. Instead, she put on a pair of latex gloves and began observing his skin. When she got to his back, she pressed her fingertips to the spot just above his left shoulder blade. "What's this?"

He knew what she saw. The intricate, black ink mark seemed to shimmer red in the light. Its patterns reminded him of a coiled serpent. "It's a spell… I think."

"You're saying you don't know what it is?"

"No." He knew it wasn't a tracking spell. He suspected it may be some sort of binding spell, but so far, he hadn't felt any side effects. He had learned enough about magic in his time with the Order to know that binding spells usually brought about side effects; nausea, vomiting, amnesia, irritability, and so on.

He felt a pair of eyes on him and he lifted his gaze.

A woman was watching him from the door. He narrowed his eyes.

Something flashed across the woman's eyes and she swiftly entered the room. "Knock, knock," she said, rapping her knuckles across the door. "Didn't start without me, did you?"

Verika looked up and tensed. "Emilia," she said with forced civility. "I thought you were in Virginia visiting your family."

"I got back early." She surveyed Elijah with cold scrutiny. Why the hell did she look so familiar? There was something about her eyes…

The woman was tall and lithe. Her dark hair was straight and came about halfway down her back. She had olive-toned skin, a white blouse and gray dress slacks. Her glasses were red-rimmed. She looked like the sophisticated, brainy type of woman. Emilia leaned against the table and folded her arms. "So what do we have here?"

"Nothing I can't handle," said Verika curtly.

"Need some help?"

"No."

Emilia's mouth quirked up. It was as if she enjoyed toying with Verika.

Elijah started to growl and then quickly stopped himself. *What the hell? She's not even your woman!*

"Well, if you say so," Emilia said, as if she didn't believe Verika could handle things on her own. She yawned and flipped her hair over her shoulder. "I'm going to grab some coffee. Want some?"

"After last time? No, thank you."

Elijah couldn't help himself. "What happened last time?"

"Oh, she tried to poison me. It was nothing a quick antidote couldn't fix."

He looked right at Emilia and gave her his wickedest smile. "Sounds like a bitch."

"Yeah, it was."

"I wasn't talking about the poison."

Emilia's eyes flashed with anger. She straightened and stomped toward the door. "Have fun with Mr. Smith. I'm sure you two will get along just fine."

She pulled at the sleeves of her blouse, which had ridden farther up her arms after she'd crossed them. Something familiar flashed along the inside of her wrist. Her watch didn't quite cover it up.

It was a pentagram with a Latin word scribbled in the middle—"Rebirth".

The Mark of the Order.

He knew Mistress Black had connections and eyes and ears everywhere. People liked to boast about that kind of power, but with her, it was legit. He'd suspected the witches had infiltrated the DPI, but somehow he didn't think he'd come across one in a city like this. It was fairly large, but there were way larger cities out there.

Terror slammed into his gut, making it harder for him to breathe.

Right before she went out the door, Emilia turned around and flashed him an evil smile.

She had *wanted* him to see her mark, wanted him to know they were watching.

Holy shit, he had to get out of here, fast.

"I need to leave," he said. "The DPI isn't as safe as you

think it is."

Verika, who had been popping the corks off vials, paused and frowned. "What do you mean?" Her eyes narrowed, and she scoffed. "Wait a minute, like, we *have a mole*? Now you're just screwing with me."

Oh, wouldn't he like to. *Get your mind out of the gutter.* He might as well accept the fact he couldn't think straight when she was around. "I'm not screwing with you. I wouldn't about something like this."

"There's no way," she said firmly. "There are spells in place to detect moles."

"And I'm sure, just like any other type of spell, that they are completely free of loopholes," he said dryly.

She paused and raised her chin. "I'm telling you it's impossible." She started to turn toward the door.

He was grasping at straws here. He needed to get her attention. *Now.* "I can help you find Mistress Black."

She froze. A few seconds passed before she found her voice. She slowly turned around, gazing at him with suspicion. "You know where she is?"

He nodded, never looking away.

She pressed her lips together, deliberating. "You're bluffing."

"No, I'm not. I know exactly where she is. But the property's bewitched so no one can ever find it. Except for me." *Liar, liar*, his conscience sang.

He could see the interest in her eyes, the intense longing to believe him.

Gotcha.

He watched the news, heard the rumors of how every

cop in the Underworld was looking for Black. Verika seemed like a fiercely loyal woman, a true cop. She'd do whatever it took to find a new lead.

She crossed her arms. "And what is the price for this favor?"

"That you break every last spell on me and promise to let me go once I take you to her."

She stared at him a beat. Then she did something totally unexpected.

With a sultry look that set his blood ablaze, she slowly approached him. He watched how her hips swayed, imagined running his hands over them.

His back pressed flat against the chair as she leaned over him, straining that beautiful neck so that her mouth hovered right above his in an almost-kiss.

He held his breath and tensed, lips parted, not realizing how much he wouldn't mind kissing her, until he found her lips less than an inch away from his.

He froze, afraid if he moved he'd ruin the moment. So he waited.

And waited.

"Forget it," she whispered, her eyes darkening. "There is no way in hell I'd ever aid a criminal."

He blinked. His breath left in a whoosh, like a balloon deflating, as she abruptly stood and stormed out of the room, slamming the door behind her.

CHAPTER FIVE

WHAT THE HELL WAS THE MATTER WITH HER?

She hadn't even done her job yet, but she'd run like hell out of that room because she couldn't stand another second around that man.

It wasn't even that she found him obnoxious or repulsive. No, on the contrary, her body had responded in an entirely unwelcome way. The way he looked at her, like he wanted her… she still felt overheated, even as she ran to the break room, grabbed a paper cup, poured herself some ice water, and chugged it. The cold liquid did nothing but make her throat hurt.

The second she'd taken his shirt off, she'd thought… *Hot damn.* It was obvious Mr. Smith had taken very good care of his physique. A landscape of hardened muscles had met her hungry gaze, and she'd found it incredibly difficult to look away from him. She couldn't get the image of his body out of her head. Worse yet, she could feel how slick her panties had gotten on the way to the break room.

It had been a long time since she'd wanted to have sex with a man. She simply didn't have time for dating and the drama that usually went with it.

Or, at least, that's the excuse she kept feeding herself. Deep down, she knew it was because she was scared of getting her heart snapped in half again. Leaving Nik had been the hardest thing she'd ever had to do. But when it became clear that he was never going to mark her, she couldn't think of a way that this could end well for either of them. In the end, she'd ultimately had to cut him loose, for both their sakes.

Verika poured herself another cup of water and gulped it down.

"Feeling all hot and bothered by Mr. Sexy Werewolf?" Emilia asked, coming up from behind her with a steaming cup of coffee.

Verika's teeth grated. This was so not how she pictured her morning going. "No. I'm just thirsty." She tried going around Emilia, but she cut her off.

Verika hated that they worked in the same department. It also didn't help that Emilia was so damned skinny. Verika was comfortable with her weight, which was a little on the plush and curvy side, but she never could quite shake the desire to wear skin-tight clothes without feeling self-conscious. And Emilia liked to show off.

Verika swore that as soon as the witch mafia case was through, she was so going to move. No more Emilia, no more bullshit. A fresh start was in order.

Emilia flashed a malicious smile at her. "Any luck

cracking those cloaking spells?"

Verika raised a brow. "Why are you so interested in this? This isn't even your case."

"It is now. The chief called me in to help you out."

Great. That stung a little. Verika made a mental note to talk to her boss once she was done with Mr. Smith. If he was losing his faith in her abilities, then she might as well pack up and transfer to a different department in another city now.

Determined not to let Emilia see how shaken up she was, Verika said smoothly, "Good. We'll get finished in half the time. I'll meet you back there in five."

Emilia's eyes flashed with anger at the dismissal. "You should be thankful a *real* witch is going to be there to supervise you, in case something goes wrong."

"Obviously, I don't require supervision, seeing as I'm a pay grade above you."

Emilia's face turned red. "For now." With that, she whirled about and marched out of the room, nearly knocking over a petite blond witch—Rosie—standing near the door.

Rosie turned a worried look toward Verika. "That must be Emilia."

"Yep." The "p" made a popping noise.

"She's… charming."

"I could think of a few other descriptions," Verika muttered darkly.

Rosie shifted her weight. "Is she giving you a hard time again?"

Verika sighed and rubbed her temples. "Yes and no.

It's nothing outside of the ordinary. It's just been a tough morning."

"I'm sorry."

"Don't be. It's not your fault." Verika smiled at her friend. "Are you enjoying your first day at the job?"

The younger girl smiled and vigorously nodded her head. "Oh, yes! It's amazing! I mean, I know I'm only a secretary for now, but I'm hoping I can move into the lab department soon."

"I'm sure you will. You always know the most at our meetings. More than our illustrious leader, sometimes."

Verika had met Rosie at her weekly spellbook club meetings. The girl was new to the area, and although she was only twenty, she was a skilled Blue Witch. Though her affinity lay with water magic, she was knowledgeable about every other kind of magic, as well as being a living and breathing grimoire. The two had started talking and soon couldn't shut up about their love for witchcraft.

Rosie blushed at Verika's compliment. "I really appreciate you getting me this job."

Verika waved away her thanks. "Don't think anything of it. We could use more people like you around here."

Rosie beamed. "Are you coming to the meeting tonight?"

"Wouldn't miss it." She really wouldn't, either. She hadn't missed a single meeting since she'd joined this past January. She'd tried online forums and stopping by local coven meetings, but most of the people she'd come across online were just humans screwing around or crackpots. As for the covens she'd visited, some were fine and others weren't. Like the one where they all practiced magic while naked. No way was she letting a bunch of strangers see her goods.

She had about given up on finding a place to fit in when a coworker referred her to the spellbook club. Finally, here were people who loved magic and loved talking about it and sharing new spells. It was different from the covens she'd visited. The club felt more academic, something her inner nerd craved. There, she didn't feel like an outcast.

Verika bid her friend goodbye and headed back up to the de-spelling rooms with a sigh.

She thought about what Emilia had said, about how thankful she should be that a "real" witch was helping her.

If there was one thing Verika had learned, it was that no matter where you went or what you did, you were always going to run into an asshole. Emilia was one of those elitist witches who thought just because a dabbler like Verika hadn't found an affinity for a certain type of magic yet, it somehow made her scum.

So what if none of the elements had ever chosen her? Her knacks so far had been in more practical magic, such as breaking spells, tracking spells, finding the loopholes other people couldn't see… It was something she'd prided herself on. She'd turned her "disability" into her greatest asset, and by doing so, had become nearly indispensable to this department. Verika knew the peers who teased her were just jealous because she outranked them. Most people respected her, though. She had to work twice as hard to compensate for her lack of a magical categorization.

The different affinities—Blue Magic, Red Magic,

Green Magic, and so on—felt a lot like cliques. She swore this place was just like high school, sometimes.

Verika braced herself as she rounded the corner. Not only would her worst enemy be in there, but she'd have to deal with Mr. Sexy again. Or more likely, her body's reaction to Mr. Sexy.

She sighed as she gripped the doorknob. *Here goes*.

She twisted.

It was locked. And the window shades had been drawn.

Verika's eyes narrowed. That bitch would try to lock her out.

Having a feeling she already knew what would happen, Verika tried swiping her badge and punching in her authorization key on the panel beside the door.

Nothing happened. It must be bewitched.

Too bad that wasn't going to work, no matter what type of spell Emilia had cast upon the security panel.

Closing her eyes, Verika held her hand up over the panel. Heat started to build below her palm as she chanted, searching for the loophole that would allow her to rip this spell apart.

The lights hummed and then began to flicker, but she ignored it. The electricity had been really weird all over the city lately. It seemed anywhere she went, lights were acting up.

Her brows furrowed in concentration as she searched the spell. She could see it in the darkness of her mind, a rainbow of multi-colored threads.

Almost… there…

Her eyes spotted the hole and she reached out with her own magic and pulled.

Her ears popped as pressure swelled in the air, and sparks sizzled beneath her palm. She gritted her teeth and jerked back her hand. Some spells didn't like to be broken, and they bit back.

Feeling cranky, she grabbed the knob without hesitation and opened the door.

"You know, Emilia, I look past a lot of your bullshit, but I'm getting really sick and tired of…"

Her voice trailed off as she took in the scene before her, and her eyes widened.

"What the hell is going on?"

CHAPTER SIX

THAT WAS EXACTLY WHAT ELIJAH WOULD LIKE TO KNOW. When Emilia had sauntered in, alone, a few minutes ago, he thought he was done for. Mistress Black would surely want him dead. He knew too much.

So, when Emilia raked a fingernail down his face and said, "She wants you back, precious," he had almost wished she had wanted him dead instead. After all, he'd bet anything the reason she wanted him back was to kill him herself.

Death at the hands of Emilia was surely better than what he was about to face.

"What do you mean, 'She wants me back'?" Elijah had demanded, despite the horror uttering those words produced.

"It means just that," Emilia had said, along with a few words that ensured the door wouldn't open. "She has big plans for you."

"What kind of plans?"

Emilia had smiled, and it had made his blood run cold. "All kinds of plans. You'll see."

"I don't want to see. I don't want to go anywhere near her again, or any of you witches, for that matter."

"Yet, your tail seemed to wag for Ms. Tate."

Damn. Was he that transparent? "You're delusional," he'd said.

"I'm a lot of things, sweet pea, but delusional isn't one of them." She'd gone over to the cabinet and grabbed a piece of chalk. With a wave of her hand, she'd barked a word in Latin and the next thing he knew, he couldn't move. She'd begun drawing a circle on the floor around his chair while he'd struggled to break free, all the while feeling his heart rate shoot up, up, up.

Emilia had started to chant as she walked. The hum of a spell had buzzed along Elijah's skin, making it prickle. The circle had begun to glow neon green.

"What are you doing?"

Emilia didn't speak again until the spell was complete. "Sending you back." She'd raised both arms, her whispered chanting growing more frenzied as her eyes became totally black.

He'd struggled in vain but couldn't move. He couldn't go back to that castle of horrors, couldn't face the terrible beauty of that madwoman again.

"Stop it," he'd breathed, but his voice was swept away in the rising gale in the room. The lights had begun to flicker. The spell had pressed against his skin, making him feel like everything was being sucked toward his torso.

He'd wondered if this is what it would feel like to be sucked into a black hole.

He'd gritted his teeth, resisting the increasingly painful pull of the spell, when the door burst open and there stood his angel. Her hair looked like fire as the wind picked it up.

"You know, Emilia, I look past a lot of your bullshit, but I'm getting really sick and tired of…"

Her voice trailed off as she took in the scene before her, and her eyes widened.

"What the hell is going on?"

Emilia whirled, fixing those black eyes on Verika. Verika startled as she took in her coworker. "Black Magic? But you're not a Black Witch."

"This power's on loan," Emilia hissed, then slashed at the air. The door slammed shut, sealing Verika inside with them. All the while, the circle still burned brightly around Elijah and the pressure increased. God, it hurt like a mother, like his insides were being siphoned out.

Verika held up her hands, circling the table so it was between her and Emilia. "Whatever you've done, you can undo it."

"Too late now. She'll kill me if she finds out I had him within my grasp and let him escape."

"Who will kill you?"

"Who do you think?" she said, lifting her arm and jerking back her shirt sleeve. The tattoo symbolizing she was a member of the Order sparkled dark red in the light, and Verika's eyes widened.

"Oh, my God," she breathed. "You're one of them." She glanced at Elijah in disbelief, as if she couldn't believe he had been right. She stared at Emilia. "You know where she is. You've known the whole time, and you haven't said a damned word."

"If you'd met her, you wouldn't either," Emilia said, along with a shiver that looked strangely like fear. Elijah could relate. Mistress Black scared the shit out of him, too.

"Emilia, let me help you," Verika pleaded.

Emilia laughed. "You can't help me. You're just a dabbler. What the hell can you possibly expect to do against someone with her power?"

Verika winced, her hurt feelings showing through briefly before pure anger took over. "I'm stronger than you think." Grabbing one of the vials she'd left off the table, she uncorked it and threw it at Elijah's feet. It burst right on the circle, causing steam to shoot up. The circle sizzled and flared before the chalk shattered like glass, leaving glowing neon green shards all over the floor.

The unbearable constriction Elijah had felt against his lungs eased, and he sucked in a huge breath, coughing.

"Bitch!" Emilia spat. "I'm sick of you sticking your nose where it doesn't belong!" Raising both arms with a cry, she shoved them outward. The table surged backward, aiming to pin Verika against the wall, but she leapt out of the way. She landed on the floor as the table banged against the wall.

Elijah instantly snarled and tried to stand, but the binding spell was still in effect. *Damn!* He hated feeling helpless, hated not being able to do anything as the world fell apart around him.

He remembered a dreary night when he'd watched in

terror as his family was turned into werewolves. He'd felt the same sense of helplessness then as he did now, as he'd watched their blood color the ground. Their screams and pleas for help still haunted his dreams.

And now, this innocent woman was most likely going to die right in front of him, all while he sat around and watched.

Furious with life continuously kicking him in the teeth, he began snarling and thrashing, trying to break free. He would not give up, not while he could still make a difference.

Verika scrambled to her feet, but Emilia seized her foot and threw her, with impossible strength. Verika crashed into the shelves of supplies, falling flat on her back and covering her head as potions, glass, and all sorts of other manner of supplies rained down on her.

"I'm so sick of hearing your name lauded among our colleagues," Emilia said as she slowly approached. "Do you have any idea how infuriating it is having someone with no clear affinity outrank you? Do you know how hard it's been smiling when someone praises you, or even just looking at you?"

Verika chuckled, the sound raspy. "If you're looking for me to apologize for your inability to control your jealousy, then sorry to disappoint you. By the way, I hope you got health insurance when you signed on." Dipping her hand into a nearby open box of what appeared to be pink sand, she quickly muttered a phrase in Gaelic and blew the dust at Emilia.

It took on a life of its own, shooting straight for her

face. She coughed and sputtered, then began to sway. "What did… you…?"

She hit the floor, unconscious, before she could even finish the question.

"Oh, my God," Verika breathed, clapping both hands around her mouth in horror. "I just stunned my coworker. Holy mother of—"

"Hey!" Elijah barked. "I don't mean to be a dick, but can you fall apart later? We need to get the hell out of here."

"We?"

He gave her an exasperated look.

Standing on shaky legs, Verika walked over to him and stared.

He waited. "Well?"

"But you'll escape if I set you free. Or kill me and *then* escape."

He snorted. "I won't harm you, I promise. But I am planning on escaping." He studied her. She was quick on her feet and obviously had some tricks up her sleeves. She could come in handy as an ally.

If you're being honest with yourself, you'll admit you just want her around so you can undress her with your eyes some more.

"You should come with me," he said.

Her breath caught. "I can't."

"Why not?"

"Because…"

"Because I'm the bad guy?" He gave Emilia a pointed look.

Verika swallowed hard and shifted her weight. "It's

just, my whole world has turned upside down in a few seconds. I have no idea what to think right now."

"Do you think I would hurt you?"

She stared back without blinking. "No."

"Do you think I would intentionally place you in harm's way?"

She bit her lip.

He sighed. "Look, I don't mean to force you into all this, but hell, you're already in the middle of it, anyway. If you're half as devoted to justice as you seem to be, then why not free me and let me help you take down the Order?"

Verika didn't reply.

"I can't stay here," he said simply. "Clearly, the Order has infiltrated your ranks, and you can take however long you like to come to grips with that. But either way, once they find me, there's no telling what they'll do to me. Now, will you please help me?"

Verika glanced at the door with indecision. "I've never broken the rules," she murmured, more to herself than anyone else. "I've never once stepped out of line. I've always been so careful. How come this is happening to me?"

"Maybe because it was meant to." He let the weight of those words sink in. He wasn't sure if he believed in fate or not, but there was something eerie about their meeting. Almost as if it was meant to be.

Verika turned her gaze back on Elijah. She muttered a few words and he could move his limbs again.

"Thank you," he said, standing quickly and looking around. He pointed to the camera mounted on the wall.

"Emilia said she spelled that to make it look like she was just de-spelling me. I think it's only supposed to last a few minutes. It's a mirage."

Verika's brows rose. "You know about mirages?"

"Yeah."

"But you're not a warlock."

"You learn a lot of random shit when you're held prisoner by a coven of malicious witches."

Verika ran her hands through her hair and began pacing. "Okay, so we need to think this through." Her voice shook, like she was trying to keep from falling apart. Her eyes fell on Emilia. "Oh, God, what have I done? I'll get fired for sure. Everyone knows we don't like each other, and she'll probably try to make it look like I just—"

Elijah took her by the arms and forced her to face him. "Just relax," he said, staring her in the eyes. "She's still breathing. She was going to attack you and you defended yourself. You have done nothing wrong."

"You're right." Verika shook her head and took a deep, calming breath. She let it out slowly. "Thanks. Sorry, lost my cool there. This isn't how I normally behave."

He somehow doubted that. Fantastic. So his witch was a control freak. Put one thing out of order in her life, and she just comes unglued.

There was no telling how she was going to act when random shit happened, but she'd handled this situation rather spectacularly, and she was sort of his only option.

They needed to act now, before they were discovered.

"Can you get us out of here?"

"I... I think so," she murmured, looking around and

seeming distracted. Her brows furrowed in thought. She began rummaging through the remnants of the potions on the floor. "Where is it, where is it…" she muttered to herself. "Aha!" She at last held up a glittering vial of what looked like bottled light.

"What the hell is that?" Elijah said, growing tense as she approached with it.

"Our ticket out of here," she said. Color heated her cheeks. "But first, I need you to hold on to me," she mumbled, not looking at him.

He quirked a brow, resisting the urge to grin. "As you wish." He stepped closer without hesitation and rested his hands on her waist.

"Um… you might want to hold on tighter." Her voice got smaller as she spoke, and the color burned more vibrantly in her cheeks.

No complaints from him. He circled his arms around her waist, enjoying the plushness of her curves. She was soft. He bet her creamy, bare skin was even softer.

She let out a startled gasp as he yanked her to him. "Like this?" he murmured in a husky voice, gazing down into her eyes.

She gulped. "Yeah," she whispered. "That should do."

Those beautiful green eyes stared up into his for a moment, searching. "What's your name? Your real name?"

He shouldn't have told her. It would have made things so much simpler between them in the long run.

But no, his recklessness kicked in, and he blurted out his name before he could think straight.

"My name is Elijah Johnson."

CHAPTER SEVEN

"**J**OHNSON?**"** VERIKA SPUTTERED. SHE COULD FEEL the heat draining from her face. She didn't need a mirror to tell her she was going white as a ghost. That name sent a crack racing through her still mending heart.

He stared at her, confused. "Is something wrong with that name? It's pretty common."

She wetted her lips and thought about what she wanted to say. Her voice cracked when she spoke. "Do you by, um, any chance have an, er, brother? Or two?"

"Yeah. Why?"

Her heart began to race. Her tongue felt heavy as she asked this next question. "Are their names Nik and Gage, by any chance?"

Now, the color drained from his face. "How did you know?"

Holy hell. She pinched the bridge of her nose, fighting the coming headache. Nothing good could come from trying to answer him right now, not when her head was still spinning with the revelation of exactly who he was. *"Oh, gee, I know because I kind of had a thing going with your brother, and you kind of remind me of him, especially the 'I-want-to-jump-your-bones' part."* Yeah, she could so see that conversation derailing quickly. So instead, she opted for, "It's a long story. Which we don't have time for right now," she added pointedly.

Don't ask, don't ask, don't ask…

He gave her a suspicious look that said he wasn't done asking questions, and that was okay. "So, about that escape spell…"

"Oh. Right." She held up the vial of Lunimora and closed her eyes, bracing herself for the magical jolt. This spell was a bitch. She'd only cast it once, while in training at the DPI Academy, and it had knocked her out cold. Her magical prowess had come a long way since, and she prayed she could stay conscious long enough to actually get them to safety.

Please, please, don't let me screw this up.

The incantation's words came to her easily enough. Memorizing spells, no matter the language, had never been hard for her. Her photographic memory probably had something to do with that. It was one of the few good things her mother had passed down to her before vanishing.

She couldn't think of those things now. She needed every drop of concentration she could muster. Wind smelling of spring and summer swirled about the room, surrounding them in a vortex. Though her eyes were closed, she could tell the room was growing brighter, and subsequently, the heat more intense.

The temperature rose as Elijah clung to her, pressing her against his chest as she struggled to maintain her grip on the rapidly vibrating bottle of Lunimora. Some said it was the soul of an angel. Which Verika thought was stupid, since she was pretty sure angels just "were" and that they didn't need souls. Others said Lunimora was bottled moonlight, or fairy magic. No one knew for sure what it was, but since its discovery in the early 1900s, it had become one of the most useful potions available.

In the midst of the swirling winds, Verika heard people banging on the door. "Don't let go," she shouted, then threw the bottle on the ground.

It sounded like a bomb went off. The de-spelling room would be a wreck. She almost worried Emilia would suffer a blow, but honestly, she didn't care. The bitch had tried to kill her.

An eye for an eye...

She had been taught better than that. Yet, she couldn't deny the dark satisfaction the thought of Emilia's too-perfect, and probably magically-altered, face getting cut up brought her.

It put a smile on her face.

Elijah shouted in surprise as they were sucked through the light-hole the potion had created and flung through time and space.

The world was a tunnel of color and light. Images and sounds rushed past them, making Verika dizzy as the magic required to cast the spell depleted her energy.

Her eyelids became very heavy, staying closed even after they'd come to an abrupt halt and had rolled against what felt like pavement.

The darkness spun behind her closed eyes, and there was a high-pitched ringing in her ears that wouldn't go away.

A deep, masculine voice that reminded her of happier times said her name from far away. She remembered calloused hands touching her face much like the ones doing so now, of a hot mouth blazing kisses down her neck, nuzzling her awake.

"Mmmmm... Nik..." she murmured, slowly coming to.

The hands froze, then removed themselves altogether. "What do you mean, 'Nik'?"

Something in her brain registered that this voice was slightly deeper, with a huskier timbre, and her eyes flashed open as her recollection of the past few minutes came rushing back. She stared up at Elijah.

Sunlight poured down around him. He hovered over her, staring at her as if she'd lost her mind. She could practically see the gears turning in his head. Neither of them breathed. Then he blinked and let out a huge breath. "Holy shit, you slept with my brother, didn't you?"

Her mouth flopped open. "I did not—that is so not—" She winced as a sharp pain struck her brain and stars sparked before her eyes. She gritted her teeth and suppressed a groan of agony. Her head, everywhere in fact, hurt so badly she could hardly stand to talk, let alone move. Well, at least she wasn't unconscious. And she knew it would be rough from the get-go, so at least she was prepared for it this time.

Always find the silver lining, no matter how much crap life throws at you. It had taken her a long time to think like that, given her tendency to be dark and bitter, but all of her self-help books had helped her turn her life around.

Elijah looked her over with a worried glance. "Are you all right?"

"Yes… no…" She struggled to shove the words out between her gritted teeth. Her hand groped along the ground before finding a brick wall. Her fingers fought to get a grip as she tried hauling herself up.

"Here. Allow me." Elijah's strong arm snaked under her shoulders, and her heart fluttered.

"Thanks," she said as he helped her to her feet. That rush of desire still lingered deep in her belly in a pool of restless heat. She had to get away from him, before he undid her completely. She took one step—and immediately found herself kissing the wall as her knees nearly gave out. Damn, she didn't remember being this weak the first time she'd done the spell. Then again, she didn't remember much of anything because she had been unconscious.

Elijah walked right next to her as she clung to the wall and began to move again. "You should lean on me," he said.

"I'm fine," she snapped, waving him away only to stumble again. Her face flamed with embarrassment. Some powerful witch she was.

"No, you're not," he said. "And unless you want to

scuff up that pretty face of yours by face-planting on the ground, I suggest you let me help you."

"I said I don't need—ah! Hey!" She gave out a surprised yelp as he scooped her up in his big, strong arms.

She wrapped her arms around his neck, her entire body aware of how solid his muscles were. She wondered what they would feel like beneath her fingertips, if his bare skin was really as delectable as it felt…

Okay, it was time for a reality check. Under no circumstances was she getting involved with another werewolf. Thanks to the whole mating Mark drama, you were almost always guaranteed to be left behind with a broken heart. Her fellow witches had tried talking her out of the relationship with Nik, but she hadn't listened. She hadn't wanted to face the truth. She'd thought that if their love was strong enough, then the mating fever wouldn't matter.

But it did. It had wrecked every hope and dream she'd had with Nik, and the knowledge that she'd been so foolish had haunted her since.

She had to be smart about this, no matter how much her body may crave Mr. Sexy's touch.

Or his mouth, or other appendages…

"You're blushing."

"What?" she gasped, blinking.

He slowly grinned. "I hope it wasn't because of me. Because then, I might start blushing."

Was he flirting with her? God, it had been so long since anyone had really noticed her like that, had made her heart flutter so… It wasn't because men hadn't tried.

It was because she hadn't let them get that close.

She cleared her throat. "Don't be ridiculous. Now put me down so we can get out of here."

Despite his protests, she wriggled and squirmed until he set her down with an exasperated sigh, grumbling something about "stubborn witches."

Keeping one hand on the wall to steady herself, she steeled her spine and forced one foot in front of the other. Although her legs felt like clay, she kept moving until they reached the mouth of the alleyway.

Elijah kept a wary eye on her at all times, until the glittering and noisy monstrosity in front of him drew his eye. He stared. "You have got to be joking. Disneyland?"

"Disney *World*, actually. Disneyland's in California. This is Florida."

He observed the palm trees. "So it is." He tentatively reached out to touch one leafy branch, as if unsure it was real. "Why here?"

Her chest tightened as she inhaled the slightly salty scent in the air, a scent she would never be able to get out of her soul. "I don't know."

But she did know. She had asked the spell to take her some place safe. It chose her homeland.

It was just as well, because she knew no matter where they went, they would never be completely safe now.

Verika sighed and walked toward the crowded parking lot.

Elijah lingered behind. "Where are you going?" he called.

"To get us a car," she said over her shoulder with a

foxy grin.

For someone who never broke the rules, she was feeling surprisingly alive.

And that, in turn, made her very daring.

CHAPTER EIGHT

ELIJAH HAD TO HAND IT TO HER—HE DIDN'T THINK SHE'D have the balls to do it. "Grand theft auto" and "perfect little witch" didn't belong together in the same sentence. Now, he ate his words as they buzzed along the highway in a new, jet-black Corvette, a stolen prepaid phone sitting in the cup holder between them.

He didn't think they were ever going to leave. She'd stood by the car, murmuring enchantments and God knew what else as people walked by staring at her like she was crazy. The Latin incantations he recognized as protection and tracing-repellent spells did wonders for encouraging people to keep their distance. At least she was thorough. He supposed it did make sense that a cop would know the best ways to avoid other cops.

This whole epic "getting captured" screw-up was starting to work out better than he'd thought.

"I could get used to this," Verika said, breaking the

long, tense silence that had stretched between them.

"Stealing shit?"

She gave him a wry look. "I was going to say the Corvette. I've never been a girl to drool over fast cars, but she sure is pretty."

For the car's outrageous price tag, she'd better be. She'd better have gold-plated rims, too. He studied Verika sidelong. Her shoulders were more relaxed and her knuckles weren't stark-white anymore. "You seem less tense."

"What gave the impression I was to begin with?"

He gave her a "really?" look. "I don't know; the fact it looked like you were about to snap that poor steering wheel in two?"

She eased her grip and drummed her fingers along the rim. "I'm always like this."

"Why?"

"What do you mean?"

"I mean… are you always this stressed out?"

"Yeah," she admitted, "usually. I don't think my body would know how to function if it wasn't under a constant state of duress."

"Sounds depressing."

She shrugged, not saying anything.

He scratched his brain for something to say. Talking to women had never been a strong suit of his, not like it had been for his younger brother, Nik. Whom she had apparently shagged at some point in time. The thought of Nik, God love him, running his paws all over Verika's naked body made him want to punch something.

Which surprised the hell out of him.

Why are you so protective? It's not like you have any claim over her.

Not that he could claim her even if he wanted to, and that was a pretty damned big *if*. At twenty-nine, his mating fever had yet to appear. Sometimes, he thought he was doomed to walk this earth alone, never to fall in love. He'd been in love before... he thought. Or, at least, what his definition of love was, based on what he'd read in books and seen in movies. He hadn't witnessed much of it first-hand since their dad had been a rowdy, abusive son of a bitch, and the Order...

He shivered, willing to do anything except think of them.

"You have that look on your face again," Verika commented, making him jump.

He ran a hand over his face. God, he needed therapy. "It's just been a long day."

"Tell me about it. My parents' house is pretty close, over in Seacrest."

He'd never heard of it, but whatever. He was just along for the ride now. Though she was what he feared and despised the most, he found himself unnervingly willing to trust her. "So you grew up here?"

"More or less." She pressed her lips together when he waited patiently for her to elaborate. "I'm adopted."

He blinked. He hadn't been expecting that. "What happened to your parents?"

She stared at the open road, her eyes distant and sad. "I don't know. I mean, my father died when I was really young, and my mother dropped me off at child services and vanished without a trace. No one's seen or heard from her since." She took a shaky breath. "And I haven't been able to find her."

With magic, he added silently. Wow. "That sucks."

"It is what it is. Fortunately, I was adopted by a nice family. I had a more or less normal life growing up… minus the magical hiccups."

"Do your folks know you're a witch?"

She nodded. "My mother always was a believer of the supernatural. And my dad grew up in the sixties, so he's cool with it." She smiled. "I haven't seen them in a while."

"How come you never went home?"

She sighed. "No time. Work always consumed my life."

He thought about asking her about what went on with his brother but decided against it. Instead, he said, "So what's your specialty?"

She immediately tensed again. "Something secret."

Oh, she shouldn't have done that. He hated secrets. With a devilish grin, he grabbed the phone up. "We'll see about that. There are no secrets on the Internet." He began punching buttons.

She glanced at him, then back at the road a few times. "What are you doing?"

"Seeing if you're on witchesandbitches.com."

"Oh, you have got to be kidding me! That site's up again? Where the hell are they basing their server now?" She growled. "I can't even count on both hands anymore the number of times I've shut down their illegal site." She smacked her hand against the wheel and growled. "Dammit, we're not supposed to post registries of witches or warlocks online. And we're especially not supposed to post their real names and powers." She leaned her head back against the seat. "If I'm not fired or demoted when we get back, I have to report this to the chief. He hates that site as much as I do."

"Do you spell your name just like it sounds?" he asked when he got to the search box, completely ignoring her woes.

She pressed her lips together. He took that as a yes and began typing. "How'd your parents come up with that name anyway?"

She looked like she wasn't going to tell him. "My mother couldn't decide if she liked Erika or Veronica more. So she married the two."

"It's unique, at least."

She snorted. "I can't tell you the number of times it's been misspelled."

"I can imagine," he murmured, scanning over the list results. She wasn't hard to find, not with a name like that.

"Verika Tate," he read. "Blood Type A, Height blah, blah, blah." He scanned the boring stats to get to the more interesting ones. "Here we go. Affiliation: DPI Detective." He whistled. "Someone's been making good grades. Type of magic—" He squinted and frowned. "Unknown? What the hell does that mean?"

"It means it's none of your business!" Verika snapped and snatched the phone out of his hand. She muttered yet another protection spell on it and tossed it back in the cup holder.

He stared at her, nonplussed. "You mean they don't

know what type of witch you are?"

Her jaw ticked and she stared straight ahead at the road. "No," she finally said with force, as if admitting so had taken great effort. "I never showed an affinity with a specific type of magic."

He frowned. That had to be tough while she was growing up. Having spent time with the Order, he knew magic was everything in their world, and affinities for a certain type of magic was crucial to social acceptance. He suddenly felt pity for her. How many taunts and jeers had she endured growing up? Did she always feel like an outcast?

Suddenly, her perfectionist nature made sense. She had something to prove, that she was just as good as everyone else.

"Eh," he said, trying to make light of the heavy subject, "it only serves to make you more unique. I don't think that's a bad thing."

She looked at him in surprise and stared. Slowly, she smiled and her eyes warmed.

Which, subsequently, caused the ice around his heart to begin to melt.

CHAPTER NINE

ELIJAH WAS BEGINNING TO SURPRISE HER MORE AND more. Given his somewhat aloof and arrogant attitude, his tenderness and understanding had thrown her off guard. Nik had been the same way... sort of. He always did things, even sympathizing, with one hundred percent effort. Elijah's method was less overwhelming and more comforting. It was nice.

She spent the remainder of their drive trying not to think about how much she was starting to enjoy his company. Or looking at him. Thanks to her earlier examination, she couldn't help but to imagine that strong, hard body of his naked..

An erotic fantasy played out in her head, one that involved her legs wrapped around his waist while he did things to her that blew her mind.

"What's that sappy look on your face for?"

She blinked, swiftly coming back to reality. "Nothing,"

she blurted. The road had never looked so interesting.

Elijah snickered and flames licked her face, as if he knew what she'd been thinking about all along.

From then on, their sparse conversation consisted of him slipping in any sexual innuendo he could. It would have been childish, if it wasn't so incredibly hot coming from those sinful lips of his.

By the time they reached a gas station, she was so flustered she could hardly think. Paying with cash, she fueled up, and off they went.

"We're going to your folks' house now?" he asked, shifting his weight. If she didn't know better, she'd say he was nervous. It was cute.

"Not yet," she said. "There's one more place we need to visit first. That marking on your back worries me. We should figure out exactly what it is." She nibbled at her lip. In truth, she already knew what it was, but she didn't dare tell Elijah for fear of worrying him further.

When she'd seen the mark shimmer dark red, her heart had nearly dropped into her stomach. Blood Magic could be volatile, worse than Black, or Death, Magic. There were so many intricacies and complications that could arise. The only reason someone tattooed someone with their blood was to link that person to them. Most witches and warlocks rarely dabbled in Blood Magic because of the serious consequences that could come about as a result of a faulty spell. All it took was one wrong symbol or mispronounced word for things to go to hell quickly.

And once you were there, there wasn't much you could do about it.

She shuddered, feeling pity and a surprising surge of anger at whoever had marked Elijah.

In the older part of town—oh, hell, who was she kidding? Every part of Seacrest was old—lay a row of mostly closed storefronts. None were well-known chain brands: Marty's Men's Shoes, Elora's Flower Stop, and so on. All locally owned and struggling to stay afloat, it seemed. Being a few miles off the coast in a remote area, Seacrest never was a popular tourist attraction. There weren't nearly as many people milling about as she remembered when her parents had brought her here as a child. It made her sad to think her hometown was slowly dying as the world moved on without it.

They pulled up to an alley and Verika and Elijah got out. Elijah looked over his shoulder at the rusting meter as he followed her into the alley. "Don't we have to put quarters or something into those things?"

"Nah. They haven't worked for as long as I can remember. I think they're just for show."

He adjusted his pace to walk alongside her. Gravel crunched under their feet, and the air smelled faintly like decay. That was probably attributed to the Dumpster hiding in the alley.

"So, where are we going?" Elijah said, glancing around. His eyes never quite lost their wariness.

Verika had never really felt sorry for the criminals she dealt with on a regular basis. Most of them were unremorseful or just plain didn't care how their actions had hurt others. But Elijah wasn't like that. She almost dared to call him a decent man. It seemed he was just a man caught up in the wrong crowd, and he was paying the price for it by never being able to feel truly safe. She pitied him that. It had to be exhausting, always being on your guard.

"We're going to an old teacher of mine," she said quietly. "She might be able to shed some light on what, exactly, you've been tattooed with. Once we make sure it's not going to come back and bite us in the ass, we'll worry about finding Mistress Black."

Elijah swallowed hard.

The shop was old, and had always looked that way. The alley was already being swallowed up by shadows, thanks to the fact it was almost dusk. Verika loved all the pretty colors in the fall but hated the shortening days.

A faded sign barely hanging on by one crooked nail read *Broomsticks*.

The new age shop was small, with a little bell that jingled as they walked inside. The sharp, sweet tang of incense, along with the lemony scent of furniture polish, burned her nose as they walked past shelves filled with different potions, books, and all other assortments of magical paraphernalia. The green and white checkered floor from the sixties still hadn't been replaced, and a violin danced through a Celtic jig in the music blaring through the little boombox situated on the register.

A rotund woman in her sixties looked up from her bookkeeping, blinked hard, and stared. A smile slowly spread on her face. "Is that my angel I see?" she said in her papery voice. She was by no means frail, though her voice had always sounded brittle. Verika had once caught a glimpse of three long scars running across the woman's throat. Her favorite childhood book heroine at the time was Nancy Drew. Wanting to be like her, Verika had questioned anyone with a connection to her mentor. All that did was bring home the fact her mentor was a recluse. So, she'd gone to the library and dug up any old newspaper articles she could find.

One was from the late 1990s about a local woman being mauled by an animal attack. A large dog was to blame. Verika remembered seeing a man hanging around the shop—a werewolf, judging from his signature—but he'd abruptly stopped showing up. Her mentor had canceled her lessons for a month after that, saying she had a "family emergency" come up.

Verika had never questioned her about the scars. Some shadows were better left buried in the past. Otherwise, if you kept breathing life into them by dwelling on them, they only grew stronger.

"Hi, Satine," Verika said, walking forward and embracing the woman. "It's been a long time."

"Too long," Satine said, still grinning. She looked at Elijah and her face paled. She took a step back, making to grab the talisman on the countertop. It was made of silver, a strong ward against werewolves.

"It's okay," Verika said, stepping in front of Elijah and holding up her hands. "He's with me. He won't hurt you, I swear it."

Satine kept hold of the talisman anyway, though at least her hand now rested by her side. She stayed a few feet away, eyeing Elijah warily. "What do you want? I assume you haven't come here to catch up."

Verika winced. Maybe bringing Elijah here was a bad idea, but she didn't know where else to go. There weren't that many people she could afford to trust. "I have a question for you." She gestured to Elijah to take off his shirt. He removed it and turned around, allowing Satine to see the tattoo.

Verika pointed to it. "Do you have any idea what this is?"

"It's a brand," Satine whispered, hand outstretched as if to touch it. Her fingers began to glow red, and the tattoo flared once her fingertips were within an inch of touching it. She hissed and abruptly drew her hand back. "It doesn't like my power. Darker magic tends not to react well to White Magic. But Blood Magic alone wouldn't react that way. Someone also used a touch of Black Magic to create this."

Verika looked at Elijah, a question in her eyes. He nodded slightly, his expression grim.

From what intel they'd gathered, Mistress Black was a Black Witch. And she had apparently branded him. But why? Brands worked in the Underworld the same way they did in the human one. They were to mark someone's property.

What the hell happened to you, Elijah?

The idea of Mistress Black thinking she owned him was enough to make Verika's blood boil. The lights in the room flickered, and the radio hissed with static.

Satine's eyes snapped to the ceiling, narrowing.

Verika looked around in curiosity and the lights and radio settled back to normal. "Odd," she murmured, perplexed. "I thought it was just in Tennessee—where I work—but it looks like that isn't the only place having weird power interruptions."

Satine was staring at her. "Yes," she murmured, shaking her head. "How odd."

Verika glanced at her watch. They'd already lingered here too long. They needed to get going. "Do you know how to safely remove this tattoo without hurting Elijah?"

Satine blinked and looked at the tattoo. Fear crept into her leathered face. "It can never be removed, only broken."

"And how do you do that?"

Satine pressed her lips together. "I don't know."

Verika's teeth ground together. "Don't know, or won't tell us?"

Satine took a deep breath. "There are some things better left untouched—"

"Look," Verika said, not in the mood for the runaround. "You said so yourself that I'm one of the most talented witches at breaking spells you've ever come across. Just point me in the right direction." When Satine didn't reply, she turned on her heel, grabbing Elijah's hand on the way. "Come on, Elijah. We're wasting our time here."

She was moving so quickly Elijah barely had time to grab his shirt.

"You don't understand what you're messing with!" Satine called. "Some doors aren't meant to be opened."

"Why?" Verika whirled, disappointment on her face. "Because my magic never chose an affinity? Because I'm not special enough, or strong enough, to handle it?"

Satine's eyes softened and she stared at Verika with

pity.

Some of Verika's anger eased. Satine had been like a grandmother to her. She was the one person who understood her magic, who never made her feel different, and had taught her to be proud, not ashamed, of who and what she was.

For her not to help…

Disappointment stung her chest, making it tight and difficult to breathe. Without a word, she slipped out of the store, frustrated at not having any answers still.

With a heavy heart, Satine watched her protégé go. Her hands trembled, had started trembling the moment the lights had begun to flicker.

Was Verika aware of the power emanating from her, struggling to be free? In all her years as a witch, and a powerful one at that, never had she before beheld a gift that massive.

Or terrible.

She knew Verika couldn't be completely oblivious to it, not when it was starting to break free of the hold put on it so long ago. Verika was choosing to ignore it, to let logic take hold, and convince her the flickering lights were nothing more than weird fluctuations with the electricity. Satine had thought the girl's mother had been exaggerating when she'd said never again would that power be unleashed upon the world.

Now *she* realized how much of a fool she had been for not believing her. Terror drove an icy spike right into her heart. What would happen when Verika found out the truth? She couldn't tell her; her mother had forbidden it. "Only train her in what is absolutely necessary," she'd said.

And so she had. And it had been enough.

Until now.

God help us all.

CHAPTER TEN

T HEY SWITCHED CARS AGAIN, THIS TIME DRIVING AWAY
in an old Camry that looked like it had seen better days.
They'd found it in a junkyard and, thanks to Verika's
magic, were able to make the engine work. Elijah had
begrudgingly let go of fifty bucks because he had bet the
witch she couldn't make that piece of shit run. Yet another
lesson learned the hard way. That was practically his
mantra by now.

"Did you tell your parents we were coming?" Elijah inquired, as they pulled into a quiet, well-kept suburb. Every
lawn was mowed and raked, with fresh coats of paint on
the houses and fall flowers bunched into expensive-look-
ing pots. It wasn't ritzy by any means, but it was a far cry
from the neighborhood he'd grown up in when he'd lived
in the city as a little kid.

"No," Verika said, as she pulled into the driveway of a
pretty two-story yellow house with white shutters and two

white rocking chairs on the front porch. "In case the DPI has the lines bugged, I didn't want to risk it."

"And they don't have other ways of spying on you?" he asked doubtfully as she pulled around back. The driveway looked like it had been added onto, stretching around back to another little parking lot in front of a storage shed. Pine trees and a tall, well-made fence surrounded the property, keeping it pretty well hidden from prying eyes.

Verika grinned as she wrenched the gears into park and the engine died with a sigh, as if relieved not to be running anymore. "Of course they do. But thankfully, I had the foresight to ward the place."

"Isn't that illegal?"

"Yeah. Sort of." She shrugged, not concerned with it.

He smiled a little. So, there was a bad girl in that angelic wrapping after all. The earlier heat at holding her in his arms—a feeling he hadn't been able to get out of his head, nor how easy it would have been to kiss her right there—still lingered south of his navel. Damn, this witch was making him awfully horny. He attributed that to the fact he hadn't seen any bedroom action in quite a while, not since he'd gotten on Mistress Black's bad side.

A tremble made his gait stiff as they walked toward the back door. Mistress Black was easily one of the most beautiful women he'd ever seen. And one of the most vicious, it turned out. But that hadn't mattered, not when he'd heard her siren song as she lured him to her bed.

"We can't stay here long, just for one night," Verika said, whispering a spell at the door. He heard a soft click and she twisted the knob. "The department thinks I've severed all ties with my family."

"Why would you do something like that?"

"To keep them safe." Her voice grew smaller, her hand lingering around the doorknob. "I couldn't bear it if something happened to them. They're all I have."

He thought about how lonely she must be. "Then why did you leave?"

Verika shrugged, hiding her gaze. He had the feeling he'd uncovered a sore topic.

"You've seen this place. There isn't much here. And there are a lot of locals who view witchcraft as being something the Devil made up." She looked at him, grave determination shining in her eyes. "My parents encouraged me to get out of here and go somewhere my gifts could be appreciated. They never made me feel ashamed of who I was."

He softened. "They sound amazing."

"They are." She opened the door and they went inside.

The back door led to the kitchen. The interior looked like a cottage. The polished wooden floors were a warm golden hue, and all the cabinetry and trim were white. The walls were all painted the same color, a paler yellow that complemented the sunny trimmings. It looked cheerful, like the house itself was filled with happiness. He wished his own home had been this way. Their father would never let their mother paint, and since she was so submissive, everything had remained in the dull, drab off-white color as when they'd first moved into their farm house.

"Mom?" Verika called. "Dad?" She waited a few seconds in silence. "Guess they're out. You thirsty?"

"No, thanks," he said, waving her away. "I wouldn't mind taking a nap, though. My body feels like it's been put through a blender."

Verika snorted, retrieving a glass from the cabinet and pouring herself some water from the tap. "Tell me about it. The side effects from the spell should fade within twenty-four hours. Here, take this." She handed him some aspirin and the glass of water. "It'll help."

He did as she said and took the tiny red pills without question. She led him up to the second story guest room, which had its own private bathroom. The place was pretty big, probably bordering 3000 square feet. It was well-kept, with polished wooden floors throughout and country-themed furniture. All the beds were covered in quilts and shabby pillows. He guessed this was what decorators called "shabby yet chic." Mistress Black, oddly enough, had been really into the home decorating networks on TV. She'd always forced him to watch whatever she wanted to watch, which had nearly bored him to death. He couldn't care less what the difference was between a quartz countertop and a granite one.

After he was situated, Verika shut the door and Elijah took off his shoes and pants—because he hated sleeping in blue jeans—before crawling up onto the bed. Not wanting to get the pristine white sheets dirty, he only folded back the quilt. He sighed. The mattress was plush but still firm, unlike the silk monstrosity Mistress Black had made him sleep in. That one had no support whatsoever and had always made his back ache in the morning, if he'd managed to sleep.

He closed his eyes and just listened. Birds chirped outside and somewhere nearby a neighbor was mowing their lawn. Drowsiness quickly settled in. It was just as well Verika hadn't taken him up on his invitation for a "buddy nap." Her face had turned a delectable shade of crimson, nearly as lovely as her hair color, and she'd mumbled excuses about putting up more wards before shutting the door.

He smiled slightly. He wondered how flustered she'd be if he kissed her neck while his hands slowly peeled away her clothes…

Something warm dripped from his fingers, drawing Elijah's blue eyes downward.

He held up his hands and gazed at his palms. They were covered in red paint. He grinned, the potion Mistress Black had made him drink at dinner making his thoughts foggy and all sense of caring scurry out the window. He'd smoked pot once, and this was akin to that high.

Someone clapped behind him and he turned to see her standing there, her figure silhouetted against the glare of the red lights she kept in her garden of horrors. He said horrors because she had statues of people and creatures she'd frozen over the centuries: demons, warlocks, witches, fairies, even angels. It was the angels she especially loved to torment. She'd always left their wings intact for the sole purpose of plucking their feathers out one by one…

"I didn't think you had it in you," she purred, her ruby lips spreading into a smile. "But you really are a brute when you put your mind to it." She raised her arms and bellowed, "Our victor, the black wolf!"

She gestured down to the ground, at the dummy he'd pounced on.

He stood there naked, having just shifted back into human form only seconds before. His mouth was slick with something warm and gooey that tasted faintly metallic. His drug-addled brain thought it was more paint, until he started to remember the moments before…

Elijah awoke with a gasp. He had no idea how long he'd been out, but he felt just as bad as, if not worse than, he did before he'd nodded off. His skin was slicked in a cold sweat.

Knowing he wasn't going back to sleep anytime soon, he crawled out of bed with a groan and went into the attached bathroom to shower.

He lingered under the hot water and steam for as long as he could, letting it erase his horrific memories and soothe his aching body. Mistress Black had been right. No matter where he ran, he'd never truly be able to escape her. She haunted his every thought, never truly letting him rest.

He both feared her power and loathed her for what she'd done to him. Someday soon, she would pay. And when she went down, it would be he who stood over her corpse, smiling.

Feeling guilty for wasting so much of the Tate's water, he quickly shut off the shower and got out. He hadn't bothered closing the bathroom door since he hadn't seen a fan in here and didn't want to steam up the room too badly.

So, when he heard a very surprised, "Oh!" from behind him, he startled and whirled about without thinking.

A middle-aged woman stood there. She was on the rounder side, wearing a simple pink cardigan, tan gauchos, and sandals. Her hair was short-cropped and as yellow as the house.

Her wide blue eyes took him in, immediately drifting downward. They widened even more. Her mouth had been in an "O" shape the entire time.

Her eyes traveled upward and she blinked hard. "I was about to call the police, but now..." She glanced down again, her eyes fluttering a few times, as if in disbelief. "Consider me ready to be pillaged."

Huh? Oh, hell! A hand flashed to cup himself as Elijah frantically groped for a towel. He went to snatch it off the hook on the wall, but it snagged. Cursing colorfully, he yanked harder and the whole hook came off, along with some wallpaper.

Shit.

This day was quickly declining into the land of epic failures.

"Mom?" Verika's voice called from the hall. He could hear her coming up the stairs, and he froze as she walked into the bedroom. Her eyes were puffy and her hair was in more disarray than it had been after the Luminora. She looked like she'd been sleeping. "What's going on...?" Her voice trailed off as she observed Elijah in all his naked glory.

Feeling an unfamiliar blush rush to his face, he swiftly covered himself with the towel.

He froze again, in what was arguably the most awkward moment of his life.

The three of them stared at each other. Verika's eyes lingered on the spot between his legs, her face slowly turning crimson. Then she blinked and words exploded out of her mouth.

"Oh, my God! Please tell me my mother did not just see…"

He grinned uncomfortably and ran a hand through his hair, nearly dropping the towel.

Verika's mother's grin was even bigger.

Verika covered her face, mortified. "O. M. G." She shook her head, her hair swishing about her. "This is so not happening. It's like something out of a nightmare."

"Oh, don't be so dramatic dear," Mrs. Tate said, patting her daughter on the back. "It's not the first time I've seen a penis."

"Please, Mother, don't ever say that word in my presence again!" The way she was squealing, you'd think she was a teenager instead of a twenty-something-year-old woman. Elijah was getting the impression she didn't handle stress very well.

"You should have told me you'd brought a guest over," Mrs. Tate said, heading for the door. "Don't forget, dinner's in an hour. We have a lot of catching up to do." She paused to kiss her daughter on the forehead. Verika peered at her mother through her splayed fingers, still covering her face with her hands. Mrs. Tate shot Elijah another appreciative look. "And do bring your friend down. I'm very interested in hearing how you two met."

With that, she shut the door, and Verika deflated. She let her breath out in a long groan and flopped onto the bed, burying her face in a pillow. "This sucks."

"Hey, it could be worse," he said, sitting beside her. "At least you didn't catch me in bed with her."

Verika lifted her face to glare at him. Her eyes shot to the slight bulge around his crotch. She blinked several times, though she didn't take her eyes off him straight away. "Could you please put some clothes on?"

He chuckled, loosening the towel a little bit to give her a better view. A satisfied thrill went through him at hearing her slight gasp as he bent over to retrieve his pants.

And found them missing.

Verika smacked her hand against her forehead. "Crap. I forgot I threw them in the washer. I'll go get you some pants." She rushed out the door and returned a moment later with a pair of blue jeans that were a little too big around the waist, a worn leather belt, and a button down plaid shirt. The clothes smelled like lavender.

"Thank you," he said, taking them from her. He gave her a foxy grin as he released the towel. It pooled at his feet. "Care to help me dress?"

Verika's jaw dropped, and her eyes once again shot straight down before she blinked and pried her gaze away. Two seconds later, she glanced back and jerked her head around. "What is the matter with you?" she said, as he swiftly dressed. "Are you some sort of exhibitionist?"

He snorted. "Hardly. I'm actually pretty selective with whom I let see me naked."

"Right, and I'm sure the number of women you've bedded isn't a mile long."

"No, that would be Nik."

Heavy silence ensued and he inwardly swore.

He gritted his teeth and sighed, as Verika grew very quiet. "Jesus, I'm sorry. That was reckless."

"It's fine," she said. "It was a long time ago." But he could tell it was anything but fine.

She pressed her lips together as more silence followed. "I should go help with dinner," she murmured and started for the door.

He didn't want her to leave. So instead, he caught her wrist and pulled her back to him.

"I'm sorry," he said, looking down into her eyes. "I never meant to hurt you."

"You're not," she breathed, sounding a little breathless as she pressed her hands against his chest. The feel of her hands rubbing up against his bared skin only served to stoke the fire growing within him. His cock was already hard, ready to show her just how much he wanted her.

He blinked hard. Even going without sex for a month, his lust was never this bad. He thought back to the first of the month, how insatiably horny he'd been. How it had gotten worse as the month had dragged on.

The full moon was less than a week away. He stared out the window, thinking. He should have recognized the signs. The mood swings, the rising lust, his desire for this *witch*, of all people…

"Oh, shit," he groaned.

"What?" Verika's head snapped up, her eyes darting everywhere. "What is it? Did the Order find us? Is it the DPI?"

"Worse," he said, his voice muffled around the palm of his hand. "My mating fever is here."

CHAPTER ELEVEN

Verika barely understood a word he'd said. "What?"

Seeing the bulky werewolf sprawled across the bed, acting like a blushing teenager, would almost be comical—if he hadn't opened his mouth after removing his hand.

"My mating fever is here."

She blinked. "Oh, is that all?"

"Is that all?" he repeated, staring at her incredulously. "Do you realize what this means?"

"Yes," she said slowly, not comprehending his distress. "But you're a werewolf."

"So?"

"So, you knew this was going to happen, eventually."

"No, I didn't," he said, jaw fixed. His eyes turned glacial with a glare. "I gave up on finding a mate."

She blinked again. "Why?"

He swallowed hard and looked down. His voice barely

came out a whisper. "I didn't think I deserved anybody, after what I did."

She watched him without moving, afraid to move in case it startled him. "What did you do? Was it that bad?" Her heart pounded in anticipation—and dread.

His eyes slowly met hers. They were lifeless, dark holes without a soul. "Terrible things, Verika. Too many horrific things you can't even begin to imagine."

A chill went down her spine. The urge to get the hell out of there struck her, and she abruptly stood. "I should go help with dinner," she said, quickly walking to the door. "Don't be late."

She shut it and leaned against the wood, her hand still gripping the doorknob.

As an agent who'd sworn to uphold the law, she should have let him keep going. Maybe Elijah himself deserved to be arrested.

But finding out he really was a criminal, and not just someone with rotten luck, would mean she'd been wrong about him.

That the guy she was starting to fall for wasn't really a prince at all. And so she'd run.

Sometimes the fairy tale was far better than the truth.

"Did you get enough carrots, Elijah?"

Elijah hated carrots but didn't protest as Mrs. Tate piled more onto his plate. "Growing boys need their vegetables," she insisted.

One thing became obvious from the moment he'd put

the first forkful into his mouth—Mrs. Tate didn't know shit about cooking. Everything tasted weird, either over-cooked and mushy or burnt and bland. She used weird combinations of spices, adding sweet to salty and any oth-er combination. His tongue was honestly worn out trying to figure out how everything was supposed to taste.

"Thanks, Mrs. Tate," he said, pasting on a smile and sticking his fork into the carrots.

Mrs. Tate beamed while Mr. Tate, a skinny, tall man with a bald head and glasses, scowled. He'd been shooting daggers at Elijah all night.

Elijah was used to overprotective fathers. He hadn't exactly been a model citizen growing up. He was the boy every father dreaded his daughter bringing home.

The bad boy.

Some of that had never left him. There were actually some days where he wondered if he'd ever grown up at all. All the things he'd done… He shuddered. To think he'd come so close to telling Verika about his past.

What would she think of him? Would she view him the same way?

He'd seen how frightened and disappointed she'd looked when she'd bolted from the guest room like a bat out of hell.

He glanced at her. She sat quietly eating, staring at her plate while she shoved tasteless peas around with her fork. She hadn't looked at him once all night, and that bothered him more than it should.

He should be thankful he didn't interest her. She was a witch, and a cop. But all he could think about during dinner was how to garner her interest once again.

"So, Elijah," Mrs. Tate said. Elijah tensed. He knew an attempt to strike up polite conversation and break the tense silence. "You said you're from the south, too?"

"Kentucky," he said, smiling.

"I've heard that's such a pretty state! I've always wanted to go, but, well, we don't get out much."

"It is a pretty state."

"Did you grow up in a city?"

He tensed.

Verika's eyes finally shot to him, taking in his posture. "I'm not sure Elijah is up to discussing his past, Mom," she said carefully.

"Why not?" Mr. Tate said, instantly on high alert. "Did you get into some kind of trouble?"

"Robert," Mrs. Tate hissed, followed by a warning glare from Verika.

"I'm just asking a simple question," he said, studying Elijah. Oh, yeah. He thought he was a criminal, all right.

"Yes, sir, actually I did," Elijah replied politely. "I often got into a lot of fights while defending my youngest brother at school. It took him a while to grow into his skin." Actually, Elijah wouldn't know because he hadn't actually seen Gage in a while. Guilt wrenched his heart, drying up his appetite.

What a shitty brother he was.

Mr. Tate's glare only sharpened. He glanced at his daughter and back to Elijah. "Must have been one brawl after another, judging from the callouses on your knuckles. Ever hit any girls?"

"Dad!" Verika hissed, with a pointed look in his direction.

Verika's reaction was sweet but unnecessary. At least Mr. Tate hadn't brought out the shotgun.

Yet.

Elijah would never forget the feeling of being caught in bed with his prom date by her parents and high-tailing it back to his truck, buck naked, while the father shot at him. Talk about good times.

"No, sir," Elijah answered, the lie rolling smoothly off his tongue. He had hit a girl, once, but Mr. Tate wouldn't understand why. He couldn't explain that the girl was a hunter who'd been about to shoot him with silver bullets.

Mr. Tate continued to stare at Elijah. "So, are you two dating?"

And the interrogation continues…

"No, Dad, we're not," Verika said pointedly. "I've already told you two this."

"You don't look at each other like you're just friends," Mr. Tate huffed.

Verika's face turned red. Elijah could tell his was doing the same, judging from the growing heat in his cheeks.

"In fact…" Mr. Tate narrowed his eyes. "You two have slept together, haven't you?"

"DAD!" Verika screeched. Elijah choked on a piece of steak and began coughing violently.

Verika shot out of her seat. "No, we haven't!" she said, flustered. "We just came to town on some business, that's all."

Silence. Both of her parents looked at their plates,

hurt settling into their expressions.

Verika sighed and closed her eyes. "I didn't mean it that way," she said weakly.

"Well," Mr. Tate said, pushing his chair back and standing up to take his plate over to the sink, "it's nice to know the only time you'll visit is when it's on official business." He smiled sadly at her. "Glad you've found a profession you really love, sweetheart." He walked out of the room, leaving thick silence in his wake.

Verika stared after him, mouth dropping open and closing again a few times. Her mother stood and smiled, though it was weak. "You and Elijah must be tired. Why don't you go on upstairs and I'll clean up?"

"Mom?"

Mrs. Tate paused to look at her daughter. Tears had started welling in Verika's eyes. One splashed down her cheek. "I'm sorry. I didn't mean—it came out wrong."

"Sssh," Mrs. Tate said, pulling her daughter to her in a hug. She caressed her thick, red hair. "I know you didn't, sweetie. It's just... we've both missed you. Your absence has been really hard on your father. You should let things cool down a bit and then go talk to him." She smiled and kissed her forehead.

Elijah sensed Mrs. Tate was equally hurt but didn't want to hurt her daughter any more. Didn't want to push her away, just in case she decided never to come back.

Verika hesitated as Mrs. Tate began clearing the table, like she wanted to help.

"Come on," Elijah said gently, taking her hand. "Let's go."

Verika glanced toward the living room, where Mr. Tate had gone. A moment later, the TV clicked on and the volume turned up to ear-splitting levels. Elijah had detected potential hearing loss in the loud way Mr. Tate spoke.

Elijah pulled Verika toward the stairs and more or less dragged her up to the second story.

They shut the door to the guest room in time for Verika to release a deep breath. She ran her hands through her hair. "I can't believe I said that."

"It was the truth," Elijah said, watching her pace back and forth. "They just took it the wrong way."

She laughed bitterly. "It's the truth, though. I do only visit when business is involved. A conference here, a case there. I've tried explaining to them why I can't come by, but they don't understand."

"They probably do," Elijah said. "But they choose to risk their safety anyway, because they love you so much and want to see you."

Verika froze and looked at him with shiny eyes. Her hands dropped to her sides.

God, she was lovely. Her lips were slightly open, as if inviting him to…

He took a step closer, and another, before he knew what he was doing. Some internal instinct was pulling him to her, and he couldn't stop, didn't want to stop.

Verika didn't back away. She stared up at him, looking more vulnerable. He wanted to wrap his arms around her and hold her close, to shield her from the world.

"You probably think I'm a horrible person," Verika said, her voice raspy. "A horrible, selfish person."

"Actually," he breathed, his heart starting to thunder in his chest, "I think you're kind of wonderful."

Then, he kissed her.

CHAPTER TWELVE

VERIKA WAS STRUCK SPEECHLESS—LITERALLY.

Every muscle in her body locked up as Elijah cupped her face, his fingers sinking into her hair, and pulled her mouth to his. The feel of his lips was like satin as he gently kissed her.

It was a question. One she answered with a primal cry of *"Oh, hell, yes"* from deep within. She didn't think. More out of instinct—and a heaping of desire—she closed her eyes and kissed him back.

Elijah groaned and deepened the kiss, guiding her over to the bed. Her back hit the mattress with surprising care as he reached beneath her to place his hand against her lower back to hold her weight. His fingers dove lower, slipping beneath the band of her pants to explore her smooth skin. She sighed with pleasure at the sensations his calloused hands sent skittering across her skin. She hadn't realized how badly she'd needed to be touched like this again, to be desired.

He broke the kiss and they both gulped down a breath. Her lips tingled, and she could already tell they'd be swollen. But to hell with her appearance. She needed to be kissed like that again. It was like fire and lust and sugar and sunshine and every other damned good thing she could think of, all collected in the sinful softness of his lips. She could grow addicted to that, to *him*.

He stared into her eyes for a second; his pupils were dilated with lust. Her heart thumped wildly in her chest as she panted, their breaths mingling. She leaned forward, aiming to kiss him, but he pulled back with a devilish grin. She was about to growl in frustration when he lowered his head and began *doing things* to her neck; sucking, kissing, nipping. Every touch brought her closer to the edge. Before long, all semblance of common sense, and the inkling this was a terrible idea, went straight out the window.

By God, it was the best bad idea she'd ever been seduced by.

He still had one hand tangled in her hair, gripping and pulling at it slightly. It sent the warm glow that had burned beneath her belly to a full-out raging wildfire. Heat flushed her skin as his fingers came around the curve of her hip to the patch of strawberry curls crowning her most sensitive area. A moan escaped her as his hand slid lower, excruciatingly slow. He moved his palm back and forth over her curls, and she began bucking her hips slightly in rhythm to the movement.

She grabbed his hand and tried guiding it lower, but he held firm. She whimpered. "Please, Elijah," she breathed.

He paused his sinful claiming of the fleshy territory of her neck to say in a husky voice, "Please what, Verika? What do you want me to do?"

"I want… I want you to touch me."

"Where?" His hand slid lower, the pad of his thumb caressing the throbbing bundle of nerves. It sent a jolt through her, making her gasp. "Here?"

"Yes," she breathed, raising her hips to meet his hand.

With sensual strokes, he moved his thumb back and forth along her sex. God, it felt so good. Every drop of tension drained out of her body. She was quickly becoming a pile of clay, more than willing to be sculpted and prodded by Elijah's very capable hands.

She could feel herself growing slicker with each gyration of her hips. Her whole body throbbed with need, begging for release.

Which Elijah apparently had plans to delay for as long as possible. He leaned in, until his lips were grazing her ear. "Tell me how you like to be touched."

Her chest rose and fell with each labored breath. "I want you…" She swallowed. Her throat was dry, making her voice raspy. "… to go inside me."

"Like this?"

His fingers slid all the way inside her. She cried out and arched her back. He slid his hand out, now slicked with her honey, and slid it back in again. And again, and again, and again, building up a rhythm. She gripped the sheets, groaning as the rising flames scorched her every fiber. She was losing her mind.

He kissed her neck, which was now slicked in a sheen

of hot sweat. "Come for me," he said.

The command was enough to drive her over the edge. She came with a loud moan of release, arching her back and bucking her hips until the sparkling tendrils of pleasure had died away. She sagged against the bed, feeling delirious as her heart raced.

Elijah's hand remained on her sex, stroking it soothingly. "How do you feel?"

Thinking after *that* required some effort. She slogged through her muddy thoughts until she found the right word. "Free."

He pondered this. "Not bad. But I think we can do better." He began sliding her pants down.

She nearly bolted upright, but he caught her by her shoulder. "What are you doing?" she asked as he gripped her panties with his other hand.

He grinned at her as he slowly pushed her back down onto the mattress. "Seeing if you taste as sweet as you smell." Before she could protest, he'd pulled her panties down enough to expose her sex, right before he planted his mouth over it.

She'd barely gotten in a breath before he began to *suck*.

She shattered, or at least, that's what it felt like. God, his mouth was a weapon that, if used in the right spots, could bring about mass destruction. He pried her legs apart as she moaned and he buried his face in her. His tongue licked her deep, searching and roving along her wet walls. Earlier had been scorching, but this was intense. All she could do was gasp and dig her fingernails into the mattress as he had her, taking her with a possessive growl low in his throat that made her shiver with desire.

She wanted this man, wanted to feel him sucking on her breasts and experience what it would feel like to have him inside of her.

The ferocity with which he made her come...

Verika nearly screamed as the second orgasm slammed into her. She closed her eyes and bit down on her lips, catching the cry of release in her mouth and swallowing it whole as she glided off the high. With a long sigh, she fell back against the bed, utterly spent. She couldn't move. Her entire body felt numb as endorphins coursed through her veins, making her lids feel heavy with sleep. She opened her eyes just long enough to see Elijah leaning over her, licking her nectar off his mouth with a grin.

She couldn't help herself. "How did I taste?" she rasped.

He bent over and kissed her. The stickiness of herself clung to her lips. "Just as I imagined. Sweet." He reached up and tenderly cupped her cheek. "And perfect."

Her heart sputtered, but it felt different from earlier. God, she wanted to kiss him. What she'd had of him, what he'd done to her... it hadn't been nearly enough. Maybe it never would be.

As her common sense began to take over, her fear also returned. "Elijah," she said carefully, reaching up to gently pry his hand from her face, "maybe we should—" Her voice abruptly cut off as she beheld the symbol seemingly carved into the skin along the back of her hand.

The lines were delicate and intricately woven in indigo ink, which seemed to shimmer faintly in the light. It first struck her as beautiful and odd, since she didn't know where it had come from.

Elijah's breath caught. His eyes were wide as he stared at her hand, features frozen in shock.

That's when she knew what the symbol was.

It was a claim—between destined mates.

Elijah had just marked her.

CHAPTER THIRTEEN

Elijah knew an oncoming freak-out when he saw one. He could smell her rising fear and hear her quickly accelerating pulse. She continued staring, wide-eyed, at the Mark.

He probably would have stared at it himself, if he had been able to take his eyes off her.

Verika was his mate. His fucking *mate*.

Holy shit. Miracles really did happen. After the things he'd done in the Order, he'd thought he'd been cursed never to find happiness with anyone. Long gone were his dreams of raising a litter with a woman he was crazy about. His deepest wish, the desire to raise a family and lead a normal, quiet life, had long since been buried deep inside his scarred heart.

But now… now, everything had changed.

He resisted the urge to reach for the woman he'd put a claim on.

He didn't know her, not very well, anyway. Did he love her? Not yet. Did she love him? That was also probably an automatic no. But already, Elijah could feel the thread between them slowly shortening, drawing them closer together toward their shared destiny.

Their meeting hadn't just been coincidence—it had been preordained.

He waited patiently for her to speak, knowing she was trying to sort out what this meant. Every muscle in his body tensed, and he hadn't realized just how much he needed her approval of him—of their bond—until she opened her mouth and knocked the wind right out of him.

"I can't marry you."

Elijah arched a brow. "I believe the correct term is 'mate.'"

"Whatever! This—" she gestured between them "—can't happen."

Carefully, he schooled his features. Showing his true feelings—that he was capable of feeling anything at all—had been used as a weapon against him in the past. It was a lesson he'd rather not repeat. "Why not?" he said casually, though he felt as if his entire existence depended upon her answer.

"Because you're a criminal! And I'm an agent of the DPI! We couldn't be anymore star-crossed if we were Romeo and Juliet!"

He chuckled. She was so cute when she was like this.

And undeniably sexy.

His already hardened cock throbbed, and his inner wolf whined, eager to make her his.

Patience, he murmured. "But I marked you," he said.

"You did. But I don't know you." She swallowed hard. "I always thought I'd marry someone for love, not because it had been arranged by destiny."

"Is that such a bad thing?" he said, sitting beside her. She didn't move away from him, which he supposed was a good sign. *Baby steps.* "I mean, I know I'm not perfect, but at least I'm not fifty with thinning hair. Plus, I still have all my teeth."

She smiled slightly, looking up at him. "Well, I suppose that's a plus," she mumbled softly, staring at her hands. Her bottom lip began to tremble.

He frowned, tucking a finger under her chin to lift her face. "What's wrong?" he murmured.

She shook her head and swiped at a tear that had fallen down her cheek. Her green eyes stared out the window. The sunshine caught the gold in them, making them sparkle.

It made his heart ache, how lovely she was. Lovely and fierce and good and kind and sexy and—

Another pang of heat went through him, and he gritted his teeth. Dammit, he didn't know if he was going to be able to control himself long enough to let her make up her mind about mating with him.

He would *never*, ever force himself upon a woman. But damn it all, this was torture.

"All my life, I've been trying to prove I was 'good enough,'" she whispered. "Good enough to be a witch, good enough to be in the DPI, good enough to be loved. But despite my efforts, I wasn't enough."

He knew instantly about whom she was talking.

She hadn't been enough for Nik.

Never mind, the whole situation had been entirely out of their control. If it had been with a friend of his, it would be one thing. But seeing as she was referring to his flesh and blood made things really freaking weird.

"You can't help it he didn't mark you," Elijah said quietly. "And neither can he."

Verika shrugged and laughed half-heartedly. "Life can be ironic sometimes, you know? Here I am, saying I've sworn off shifters because nothing good can ever come from loving one."

He winced.

"Loving a werewolf means heartache. In your universe, love has rules. Spells and magic choose whom you love, rather than your heart. And I was tired of having mine torn into pieces."

Elijah studied her. "Nik wasn't the first shifter you'd dated."

Verika smiled sadly. "Nope." She made a popping noise on the "p". "Guess you can say I have a thing for them."

"So, you're drawn to bad boys." He grinned.

She flushed and looked away. "Well, as you can see, I'm not such a saint myself."

"I think you're perfect," he said, reaching up to wrap a strawberry curl around his finger. Her hair was soft, and a rich, dark red that artificial hair color could only dream of matching.

She looked at him then, searching his eyes, as if his compliment surprised her. Hell, it had sort of surprised him.

What was that you were saying about staying away from witches…? a snide voice in his head said.

"How long has it been since you've spoken with your brothers?" she said.

He blinked. Talk about out of the blue. "Too long," he admitted, his jaw ticking. He wasn't angry at them, rather at the whole damned situation he was in. Leave it to him to land himself in a whole steaming pile of trouble.

"Why?" she asked. The question was nonjudgmental, more curious than anything.

He shook his head, heaviness settling into his heart. "I didn't want to drag them into the whole mess with the Order. I couldn't risk their lives like that. I've already failed them by abandoning them and not looking after them like I should have."

"It's not your fault," she said gently after a moment.

"Isn't it, though? They won't understand abandonment."

"Maybe they will," she insisted. "You won't know unless you try to reconnect with them."

He winced. God, he wanted to so much. Any feeble hope he felt was soon squashed. "Doesn't matter now, anyway," he said bitterly, gesturing to the tattoo on his back. It hadn't vanished when he'd marked Verika. He could still feel its evil vibe pulsing through his skin like a sentient being. Always watching, always waiting. "I'm probably never going to be rid of her," he said, glancing at her with fear. The next words were incredibly hard to spit out. Not one to be a pussy, he sucked it up and did it anyway. "You don't have to mate with me. I'll understand if you want to leave and never see me again." He chuckled darkly. "I'll bet you're wishing you'd never met me."

"Elijah," Verika gently chided. She sighed and ran her hands through her hair. "Right now, I don't know what to think. It's all happening so fast." She pressed her lips together and tapped her nails on the bedspread. "I know the mark can't be undone." She took a deep breath, let it out. "I'm going to change into a werewolf two new moons from now, whether I want to or not." There was no bitterness about her statement, rather a statement of the facts.

She looked at his back, eyes sparkling. "Though my fate may be unchangeable, that doesn't mean yours has to be." She smiled, but there was tightness to it. "I may have an idea to break that brand. But first, we're going to need some supplies."

CHAPTER FOURTEEN

CONSIDERING IT WAS GETTING DARK AND EVERY PLACE around here closed when the sun set, they had to shimmy out the door.

Tense silence blanketed the car. Verika had turned on the radio, but it still felt awkward. Somehow, the music almost accentuated the fact things were tense between them.

No, scratch "tense" and jump straight to "holy shit what the hell is happening?"

She knew she'd dodged his unspoken question when he'd told her she didn't have to mate with him. Truthfully, she didn't know how to answer him right now.

Do I want to be his mate? Do I want to be bound to him forever?

Some people dreamed about that kind of love, of a bond that went soul-deep. She certainly had, as a little girl, and hell, even into her adult years. She'd thought all those dreams had been shattered when she ripped out her own heart by walking away from Nik. Without a doubt, it had been the hardest thing she'd ever done in her entire life. There was never an easy way to say goodbye to someone you love, despite knowing that love wasn't good for you.

Verika had known it was only a matter of time before Nik marked someone. He swore he'd disregard the Mark, that his heart only belonged to her.

She'd wanted to believe his promises. She'd wanted to believe that a love that strong was unbreakable.

Not only was it *not* unbreakable—it was fragile. She knew better than most just how strong magic could be. Not only could she sense the inevitable heartbreak they'd both experience, but she hadn't wanted to put him or even his future mate in that position. It wouldn't have ended well for anyone, and she'd loved him too damned much.

So, she'd done the only thing she could do.

She'd walked away and sworn off shifters ever since.

That is, until the delectable male in the passenger seat stormed into her life.

She swallowed the lump in her throat as they pulled up to the convenience store and got out. Elijah hadn't said a word on the way over. For that, she was grateful. She didn't want to talk about what had just happened between them, didn't want to believe her developing feelings for him were solely due to the fact she was his mate.

Or future mate, she corrected herself.

Elijah smiled at her when she caught his gaze from across the car. His smile was easy enough, but his eyes were weighed down by sadness.

And fear.

A shiver went through her, and the lamppost over-head flickered for a second.

Verika barely noticed it, though Elijah's head shot up. He frowned.

"Come on," she said, hugging herself, though it wasn't very cold out. "We should slip in while it's not crowded."

His eyes lingered on the lamppost, which had gone back to normal, before he followed her into the store.

It looked the same as any convenience store, with aisles of candy, drinks, over-priced drugs, and chips. It smelled of roasting hot dogs and freshly mopped floors. The sterile fluorescent lights exaggerated how clean the place really was. There wasn't so much as a speck of grime or dust. In fact, it was freakishly organized, as if they'd never had any customers.

Verika largely attributed that to the fact it was owned by OCD vampires.

She approached the counter, where a tall, gangly teen in a hot pink T-shirt that said FUCK TEAM EDWARD. I'M ON TEAM DRACULA stood. He popped his gum, looking for all the world like he'd rather be cleaning the toilet than manning the register.

Elijah growled softly behind her as the teen's eyes appraised her. She gave him a wry "stand down" look and rested her elbows on the counter, leaning forward. "I'm looking for that True Blood knock-off drink that's so popular right now. Everywhere else is out, but I'm told you guys have it. Where can I find it?"

His eyes flashed red for a split second, and he smiled.

His teeth looked sharper than a normal human's would. "Check in the back," he purred, still eyeing her in a way that made her flesh crawl. "There should be some extras in there."

"Thank you," she said, forcing herself to smile politely and walk away as calmly as possible. Running from a vampire was just asking for trouble. They were predators who loved the thrill of the hunt.

Deaths related to vampires had been a rising problem the past decade. Thankfully, there were now more laws in place to help keep them leashed.

Elijah glared at the vamp as they walked toward the back storeroom.

It was roomy, with crates and cardboard boxes stacked in neat columns throughout. A man in a flower shirt and jeans stood there taking inventory. He looked up and smiled when he saw her. "Ah, officer. How can I be of assistance?" he said smoothly, discreetly covering up whatever he had been working on by leaning forward and resting his elbows on the boxes.

"I need blood," she said bluntly, not in the mood to screw around.

He blinked, taken aback. "Oh, there is no blood here."

"Come on now, Dawson. I know better than that. Your lackey out front even said there was some back here when I used the code phrase we've picked up on the streets."

He tensed, his eyes glowing red. "Insolent brat. It's so hard to find reliable help these days. Everyone's an idiot."

"Relax," she said dryly. "I'm not here for a bust." She crossed her arms. "I'm here for business."

He raised a brow, intrigued. "What kind of business?"

"The kind that involves you keeping your mouth shut about it." She glanced at his papers, a thinly veiled threat. *Or else, I'll turn your little illegal dealings in human blood in to the DPI.*

He bristled, a catty smile spreading across his lips. "Fair enough. What do you want?" he said, dropping the civility.

"I need a bag of every blood type you have," she said. "A quart should do."

He appraised her. "That's not cheap."

"Neither is my silence about exactly what type of convenience store you're running."

He went utterly still, sizing her up.

Elijah tensed, looking like he was bracing for a fight.

Dawson glanced at the towering werewolf. A werewolf bite was lethal to a vampire. And Dawson might be immortal, but his beer gut and general lack of muscle tone suggested he wasn't nearly a match for Elijah…

"Let me get that for you," Dawson said, faking a smile. "I'll be right back."

He took his inventory with him and scampered off.

Elijah let out a breath and stared at her with both brows raised. "You're blackmailing a vampire? Really?"

"If it suits me," she said idly, shifting her weight. Her boss would kill her if he ever found out. She'd definitely lose her badge for sure.

Was it worth it?

She didn't even have to think twice about it. If it could help Elijah, she'd do just about anything.

Which, in and of itself, was ludicrous.

Heat kissed her skin, and she became aware of his arm brushing hers.

He was entirely too close. And yet, as he took her hand and pulled her around to face him, she found she couldn't pull away.

Her body wanted to touch him, to feel his hands and mouth moving over her as it had earlier.

Heat rushed through her cheeks and she clenched for him.

Ugh! Why did he have to have this effect on her? Why, oh, why, did he have to be a werewolf?

"Why are we really here? What are you up to?" he said, dark mischief dancing in his eyes.

"Nothing," she said quickly, making herself look into his eyes. *Challenge accepted.* She would not be intimidated by him, no matter how intolerably sexy he was.

"Are you doing this for me?" he asked after a measured second. His fingertip traced a path up her arm and across her shoulder blade, making her heart race.

"No," she lied. Swallowed. "Yes."

"Why?"

"I don't know," she admitted.

He leaned in, his breath hot against her ear. His dark voice stoked the rising fire within her. "Is it because you've decided to surrender to me? To be mine, forever?"

She couldn't breathe. Couldn't think. Her heart hammered inside her chest as her thoughts spun, and she struggled to form an answer.

She didn't argue as he pressed her back flat against

the wall, pinning her wrists to the cold cinderblock. Her mouth opened as he pressed his hot lips to hers, eagerly inviting his tongue to explore her mouth. He kissed her deeper, making her moan with longing. One of his hands slid down her neck, trailing down her chest to glide over her breast. Its descent stopped there as he cupped it and squeezed.

She sighed, rubbing her breasts against his hands. He began kneading them, and a moan caught in her throat. Her eyes drifted closed as she gave in to the moment. Oh, she wanted sex right now so badly, wanted *him*.

"I could show you passion," he breathed against her neck. His hand climbed down the curve of her hip, slipping inside her pants to tease the soft hair above her sex. "I could show you devotion and loyalty and do anything in my power to make you happy. You say this can't work, but you know what I really think? I think you're just too scared to give us a try."

Her eyes flew open. Was she that afraid? The mere mention of getting involved with another man was enough to make her tremble.

He gently touched her sex, and her breath caught as he tenderly kissed her neck. "I'm rough around the edges, but I'm worth learning to love. Let me show you I'm worth taking the risk for."

Her breathing deepened as she stared at him, a silent question written in his eyes.

A throat cleared, and they leapt apart.

Dawson stood there eyeing them with a cheeky grin. "Is this part of the good cop or bad cop routine?"

She glared at him, her face flushing. "Do you have what I asked for?" she said coolly, not giving him the benefit of knowing he'd rattled her with the dig.

He brought it over and she inspected the bags. She gave him one last level glare. "Remember what I said, earlier. You keep your mouth shut, and I'll keep mine shut. Deal?"

"Fine, fine," he snapped, shooing her away. "Now get out before you decide to rip me off some more."

She handed some of the bags to Elijah, which he tucked inside his jacket. She tucked the others inside her purse.

Elijah hadn't stopped looking at her as they walked back to the front of the store. It was only making her more on edge, but in a good way.

It wasn't until they were in the car and on their way back to her parents' house that he said, "So, you going to tell me what the blood is for?"

She took a shaky breath, trying to keep a grip on the leather steering wheel despite her sweating palms.

"You'll see soon enough."

CHAPTER FIFTEEN

Elijah was starting to freak out. Nah, screw freak out—make that about to lose his damn mind.

Verika had been staring at his naked back for the past ten minutes. Since walking through the door and locking themselves in the guest room, she'd remained tight-lipped.

Now, when a woman dragged him into a room, he expected to hit the bed with her within a minute. His sex had gotten super-excited when she'd ordered him to take off his shirt.

Unfortunately, nothing had come from that command other than long, silent minutes. The tension stretched between them like a cord.

"You made up your mind yet?" he asked. The only hint she'd given him as to what the hell she was up to was that she "had an idea and it involved a spell."

That part had made him start sweating bullets, but

he wasn't about let on to that. He wouldn't be able to call himself a werewolf if he admitted to being a pussy around incantations and candles. The stuff gave him the creeps.

Fucking magic.

Verika didn't reply for a long while. "I'm scared."

He snorted. "That's comforting."

"No… ugh!" She sighed and rubbed at her eyes. They were starting to look dry from staring at his back for so long. "I mean, Blood Magic can be unpredictable. I can't guarantee there won't be side effects in my attempting to remove your brand."

So that's what she'd been thinking of. He'd suspected, of course, but he was having a hard time reading her. The shields surrounding her feelings were nearly as impenetrable as his own.

He tried to sound nonchalant as he said, "It can't be any worse than the spells I've already survived."

Verika shuddered. "Yes, but I'm still hesitant. I could seriously injure you if I don't get this right."

He gave her a wicked grin. Almost as an afterthought, he brushed away a stray piece of hair from her face. Her breath caught as he leaned in. "Do your worst," he whispered in a sultry challenge.

He briefly glanced at her lips. They were parted, as if inviting him to explore them further. With great resolve, he pulled back and forced himself to turn around.

He smiled to himself as he heard Verika release a long breath. "I have to be out of my mind," she said.

"For thinking I'm so sexy?" he inquired lightly, over his shoulder.

She shoved him. "No. But nothing short of insanity could possess me to attempt a spell this dangerous." Another deep breath. This time she sounded more determined. "But Satine always said that in witchcraft the old adage is true; to fight fire, you need fire… or in this case, blood."

He swallowed hard. "I'm ready when you are. I'm not afraid… I trust you."

She went still, not even breathing.

Slowly, without another word, she pressed wet fingertips against the brand. He knew from the zing that went through him that she had dipped her fingertips in the first bag of blood. Since he had no idea what blood type Mistress Black was, Verika said she'd have to try each type to see which one the brand responded to.

He couldn't wait.

Verika began chanting. His heart leapt to his throat. Chills broke out over his skin, and he could feel the first strands of panic creeping in.

Relax. Calm down, he willed himself. He forced himself to focus on his breathing and closed his eyes. *Deep breath in, long breath out. Deep breath in…*

He vaguely felt her touch leave, only to return a moment later with new blood. He was taken with trying to keep from thinking about the spell she was casting on him when a lightning-hot zap went through him, ripping apart his brain and sucking him into his vilest memory.

He could barely see or hear, for the drugs in his system.

Another game was about to commence, another test to see if he was fit to be Mistress Black's guard dog.

To be her slave.

Laden with so much poison, it was nearly impossible to fight back. A toddler would have had more strength of will. The spell made him hallucinate as the swish of long skirts reached his ears. A woman came into view, the skirt of her dress moving like smoke and shadows.

"It is time, my pet," said the silky voice he had once thought sexy and irresistible.

God, he'd been such a fool to trust her. A reckless thrill-seeker. That's what he was. A damned fool. Never could resist hot women, even when he knew they were bad for him. But by the time he'd realized he'd stumbled into the viper's nest, it was too late to crawl out. He belonged to her, body and soul.

He couldn't protest as she waved her hand and the magic sizzled over his skin. The chains that had secured him to the wall of the dank dungeon fell to the floor. Her face was encased in shadows, but he heard the smile in her voice as she crooked a long, pale finger. "Come."

His body couldn't refuse. Mechanically, he followed her up the stairs and through the long stone corridor that led to the arena. No, not the arena—a forest.

Torches were lit in even intervals along the trees, seeming to hover in the darkness because it was so thick.

"I have a special treat for you tonight," Mistress Black purred, stroking his hair as if she were petting a dog. That's all he'd ever been to her—an amusement, a pet.

Fucking bitch.

A howl sounded in the distance, and his inner wolf stirred. All his senses went on high-alert. He knew that sound, remembered it tangled in his brothers' screams from his nightmares about the night they were all bitten by a werewolf.

"Yes," she murmured, still stroking him. "You recognize your old enemy, I take it?"

A growl was his response.

She chuckled. It sounded cold and brittle. Sinister. Her lips were beside his ear as she commanded with quiet authority, "Go and claim your prey. Take the vengeance that should have been yours the night those assholes ruined your life."

He didn't need any prodding. The change came in an instant, his inner wolf snarling free in a flash of snapping bones and glistening teeth. He tore through the woods, Mistress Black's laughter echoing all around him.

He could smell his prey, just a short distance away. Its fear was palpable, and he licked his muzzle. All the nights he'd dreamed of tasting this son of a bitch's blood...

Feet pounded the ground in front of him. They were slow and bulky.

Human feet.

Mistress Black must have enchanted him to remain in his human form. Her cruelty truly knew no bounds. Most of the time, he feared and loathed her, but tonight he loved her.

Tonight, he would finally make that man pay, the one who had taken everything from him.

The thirst for blood wrapped around his senses,

driving him forward. Faster and faster he ran, until he was upon the man in a blur of black fur. The man screamed, his terrified eyes staring up into Elijah's for a brief, satisfying second.

It felt so damned good to see him so scared.

Without a second thought, Elijah tore out the man's throat.

The woods abruptly faded, revealing an arena filled with black-cloaked figures. Torches lined the tall, stone walls, and blood soaked the ground at his paws.

Mistress Black stood at the center of the raised dais designated for high-ranking Order witches and warlocks. A black veil cloaked her face, but her ruby smile shone through the intricate lacework. "Well, done, my pet. Very well done, indeed."

Applause filled the arena as he backed away, whining in confusion. What had happened? Where did the woods go?

People began to stand, chanting something in an ancient language.

Someone whistled their approval. Elijah looked up to find a regal man standing beside Mistress Black.

He'd seen enough pictures to know the High King of Werewolves when he saw him.

His heart began to pound, and he lost control of his inner wolf. He shifted back, standing there naked and shivering in the sudden cold. Blood covered his hands. He held them up, watched as the moonlight glistened off them. There was so much blood that it dripped off his hands and splashed against a puddle at his feet.

With dread, he looked down.

A sob tore from his mouth.

A child, a witch, lay at his feet. He'd heard Mistress Black raging about her, how "promising a White Witch" the High Council had praised her to be, and how she was going to snuff out her light like a candle, before she became a threat.

And she'd done just that, using Elijah as the killing blow.

The people began throwing coins at him.

Entertainment. They thought this was entertainment.

Rage and horror mixed within him, swelling as he pressed his hands against his ears to drown out their applause.

He gritted his teeth, the tension in his body humming and vibrating, ripping apart his human shell as the enraged wolf spilled out.

The next thing he knew, a woman was shouting his name. He opened his eyes to find massive black paws pinning Verika against the floor, his jaws wrapped around her throat.

CHAPTER SIXTEEN

I T TOOK ALL OF TWO SECONDS FOR THE HAZE OF HIS terror to fade. Part of that could be attributed to the bedroom door flying open, followed by a blood curdling scream of horror-movie proportions and the crank of a shotgun barrel. Abruptly, he shifted back and got off Verika, about the time her father jerked the barrel in his face.

"Get the hell out of my house, monster," Mr. Tate said in a low voice, eyes never once blinking.

"Dad," Verika said, scrambling to her feet, but Elijah held up a hand to cut her off. She glanced nervously between them.

Elijah didn't even care he was buck naked. Not getting a hole blown in his head was a high priority right now. He held up his hands. "Take it easy."

"Take it easy?" Mr. Tate said incredulously. "You were about to rip my daughter's throat out!"

"I know what it looks like," he said cautiously.

"I do too. Now get out. You won't get another warning."

"It was my fault!" Verika interjected, getting between the barrel and Elijah. Elijah instinctively stepped forward to put her behind him and out of harm's way, but she waved him off. "A spell backfired and it triggered the change. He would never hurt me."

Elijah stared at her. So much trust, in so little time. He suddenly felt unworthy of her faith in him. If she knew the darker part of his soul, she'd run screaming from him and never look back.

"It sure as hell didn't look like that when he had his jaws around your throat," Mr. Tate said, shooting Elijah a glare that could melt flesh. "He's dangerous. I could see bad news written all over him the second I laid eyes on him."

"Dad—"

"And I want him out of my house right now."

Verika pleaded with him with her eyes. "Please don't do this."

"It's already done!" He shoved Verika out of the way with the barrel and aimed it at Elijah. "You have ten seconds to get some pants on and high-tail it out of here before things get messy. One…"

Elijah knew that murderous gleam, had seen it on plenty of angry fathers' faces. Not wasting any time, he grabbed a nearby pair of pants and awkwardly put them on while doing some weird hop-skip-jump step toward the door. Thank God Mrs. Tate had brought up extras. She must have assumed they'd be staying longer.

Verika trailed after Elijah. Her father paused long enough to tell her to stay put, a command she promptly ignored. His counting sped up, as did Elijah's steps. He had never been more appreciative for werewolf grace. Without it, he would have tripped down the last few stairs as his pants leg got caught on his heel.

"You don't have to go," Verika said, as they cleared the stairs. "It's not the first time he's lost his cool. I'll talk to him."

Elijah grinned. "Appreciate it, sweetheart, but something tells me he's not going to cool down anytime soon. And I don't intend on becoming a rug."

"You won't become a rug," she muttered, then winced as her father yelled at her to stay put. "Then again…"

He stormed into the kitchen, right behind them. Mrs. Tate fluttered behind, hands waving and looking completely distraught.

Elijah gave her a small smile. "Thank you for your kindness."

"It's more than you deserve!" Mr. Tate snapped.

"Dad!" Verika hissed.

Elijah gulped. Grabbing the doorknob, he opened the door. Verika made to follow him, but her father grabbed her arm.

"You're not going anywhere!" Mr. Tate roared.

She jerked free of his grasp. Elijah swore the shadows flickered and shifted in the room, but it could have been the aftereffects of the spell. "I can't leave him alone."

"Like hell, you're leaving!" her father roared, charging after her. "No way is a daughter of mine going with that low-life, son of a—"

"He's my mate, Dad!" she screamed.

That stopped him dead. He stared at her, the gun lowering. "Your… your *what*?"

Elijah stopped breathing. Verika stared down her father. "It's true. He marked me."

"What the hell does that mean?" Mr. Tate said, his face jerking back and forth between them, as if that would reveal the answers.

Verika gulped. "It means I'm going to marry him."

Elijah's heart stopped beating. He swore it did. Either that or the words "marry him" broke his brain.

The Tates stared at their daughter, jaws open and eyes wide. There was about a beat of silence before questions burst from their lips. Well, questions from Mrs. Tate's lips. Mostly profanity and objections spewed from Mr. Tate's lips.

"Are you out of your damned mind? He tried to kill you! No daughter of mine is going to marry some—"

Verika shook her head and shouted, "I'm sorry! I'll come back and explain," before heading out the door.

She had enough sense to grab her purse and keys before leaving. They got in the car and drove off.

A few minutes of silence passed as they each absorbed what had just happened. Elijah glanced at her. Her hands gripped the steering wheel so tightly her knuckles were turning white.

He held back from touching her, no matter how much he wanted to. If he did, she might shatter. "You okay?" he asked gently.

She blinked and startled, then took a deep breath. "Yeah. I'll be fine. It's not the first screaming match I've gotten into with my dad." She chuckled, a broken, feeble sound. "Our temper tantrums are legendary."

"You stood up for me." A pause. "Called me your mate."

She lifted her head and looked at him. "Yeah, I did," she said softly.

The question burned on his tongue. *Did you change your mind about wanting to mate with me?*

He wasn't ready for the answer, not yet. Better off pretending things could actually work out between them. She was right. They really were star-crossed.

Absentmindedly, Verika reached into her purse and fished around for her phone. She frowned when she checked the screen.

"What is it?" Elijah said, immediately tensing.

"It's Satine." Verika scrolled through the messages. "I have fifteen missed calls. She must have found a way around my wards to be able to call me. No one knows this number."

"Did she leave any messages?"

She checked. "No." Her nails drummed along the steering wheel.

"You want to go check on her?" he asked.

She took in a breath and let it out. "We should. I have a bad feeling about this."

That makes two of us.

They drove in tense silence to the shop. He never left her side the entire time to the store.

Nothing looked out of the ordinary, yet every sense screamed at him to get out. It wasn't so much physical evidence that something was amiss as it was a sensation, a warning lingering in the back of his mind.

"Something's wrong," Verika said quietly as they walked through the store. The stereo was still blaring classical violin, and incense burned from a jar in the corner.

That's what made it so hard to pick up on the smell of freshly spilled blood.

Elijah growled and bared his fangs as he grabbed Verika and yanked her close. "Someone's been here... a werewolf."

"Satine," Verika breathed, her face paling. She scrambled to get free of him, the lights and shadows flickering.

His heartbeat faltered with fear, just long enough for her to slip from his grasp.

He raced after her, crying her name as she ran to the back room where all the supplies and inventory were kept.

He didn't have to hear her horrified sob to know what he'd find—Satine, broken and bloody on the floor, in a pool of her own blood.

CHAPTER SEVENTEEN

BLOOD. SO MUCH BLOOD EVERYWHERE. ON THE FLOOR, splattered on the walls, in a lake beneath the almost unrecognizable body of her mentor…

The world spun. She ducked her head just in time to avoid depositing her guts onto Elijah's bare feet.

He held her hair back, rubbing one hand up and down her back in soothing strokes. God, it stunk in here. It smelled of death and agony.

She couldn't bring herself to look at Satine. The image of the angry lacerations that had been carved into her skin was burned into her mind.

Satine was peaceful, having long removed herself from the cutthroat politics of the witching world despite the fact she was extremely powerful. All she'd wanted was to live a quiet life. Who would want to do something like this to her?

Verika straightened, catching her breath and

concentrating on keeping herself from falling apart.

"Are you all right?" Elijah asked, his handsome features etched with concern.

She swallowed, her throat tasting vile and scratchy. "Yeah," she rasped, wiping her mouth with the back of her hand. "Just shocked."

He grabbed her arms and tried directing her back to the door. "We should go."

"No." She stopped him and he reluctantly let her go. Bracing herself, she stepped past him and forced herself to examine the body with the emotional detachment of a DPI agent.

What looked out of place? What unusual traces did the attacker leave behind? Her training kept running through her head, helping her to keep calm.

"It can't be a coincidence I had so many missed calls and then this happened," Verika said. Her voice was starting to regain some of its strength.

"Do you know anyone with a vendetta against her?" Elijah asked, surveying the grisly scene.

Verika sighed. "No. Not really, anyway. She was pretty much nice to everyone and well-respected in the witching community. She kept to herself a lot. Didn't want to fool with all that 'political bullshit,'" she added with a sad smile.

Elijah studied the body and the surroundings with a critical eye. "It was definitely a werewolf. They tried to hide their signature but did a pretty shitty job of it."

"How can you tell?"

He shrugged, looking away. "I've had a lot of practice."

She knew it had something to do with what had

happened to him when he was detained by the Order. His screams from when her spell had backfired still haunted her. She caught the name "Black" from his mumbling and figured he was reliving some unpleasant memory. She wouldn't push him to talk about it. When he was ready to open up to her, he would.

Not pressing the subject, she said, "Do you recognize the werewolf scent?"

He sniffed again and shook his head with a growl. "No. I can tell you I don't know him."

Verika's shoulders fell. This was all such a mess. "Does Mistress Black keep any werewolves on her payroll?"

"Oh, yeah. That and fairies and angels and demons and all sorts of other creatures she thinks might come in handy."

Verika wanted to punch something. How many people did Mistress Black have on her payroll? How many government officials, doctors, lawyers, thugs, DPI agents? How many people had slipped under their radar?

"No one should have that much power and sway," Verika said with a shudder.

"Especially a psychotic bitch like her," Elijah muttered, eyes flashing gold.

Verika sighed, biting her lip to distract her from the tears stinging her eyes. "We should call the police."

Elijah studied her. "But you don't want to."

Verika nibbled her lip. "It's hard to trust people to take care of her body. What if they also work for Mistress Black and just try to get rid of the body by any means necessary?"

Elijah searched her eyes. "Then let's not call the DPI."

Indecision warred in her. She should uphold the law. After all, she'd taken an oath.

Look at how many rules you've broken so far. And you call yourself an agent?

Her instincts told her to keep this quiet, that even people she thought she could trust could be the enemy.

Feeling like a rotten cop, she opened her mouth to speak when Elijah's head jerked to the side. His eyes widened as he sucked in a breath.

"Get—"

The building shook with an eardrum-splitting boom. Verika was nearly thrown into the wall, but Elijah caught hold of her before she could crack her head on the cement.

"You okay?" he said.

She nodded. "What the hell was that?"

"Don't know. It sounded like it came from the alley."

Taking her hand, he led her out through the store and into the alley.

Smoke billowed through the door, sending them both into coughing fits. Big, dark gray clouds and flames billowed out of what used to be her car. Or, well, someone's car, considering it was stolen.

Chills ran up her spine. It had to be whoever killed Satine. Had they been watching them when they'd walked in? How close had they come to death?

"Verika."

Her eyes snapped to the side as Elijah pointed to the door. A piece of paper had been tacked there. A message that appeared to have been scrawled in blood glared on the white page.

If you want answers, come to your parents' house, little witch.

—G

She nearly choked on her own heart as it leapt to her throat. "Oh, my God. My parents! I can't lose them. I can't." Her hands started to shake.

Elijah grabbed her and made her face him before she could fall completely apart. "It's going to be okay. We'll get to them."

"How?" Verika gestured at the car. "Even if I ghetto-rig it with spells, I doubt it's going to run."

He grinned. "Who said anything about taking a car?"

The way back to her parents' house seemed to take forever, but that could have been the fact she was holding on for dear life on the back of a gigantic black wolf.

Elijah was surprisingly swift for his size. His muscles moved beneath her, sure and strong. She'd cast a cloaking spell so no one would see them. Not that they'd believe what they saw. When was the last time anyone saw a crazy redhead riding a wolf like a horse?

Elijah skidded to a halt outside her parents' house, right in the back where it was shielded from prying eyes. He shifted back, grabbing the cloth off the picnic table to cover himself, and they charged the door. It was wide open. Immediately, she sensed a werewolf.

Elijah growled as a tall, dark figure came from the kitchen.

He was handsome, with wildness in his eyes that

clashed with his well-dressed exterior. He was tall, like most wolves were, and his leather jacket showed off his broad shoulders. Honestly, what was it with werewolves and leather? His clothing looked high-label. The jeans were new, as were the black boots with silver spurs. His dark hair had been combed back with a bit of gel. Verika might have found him handsome had she not known what he was capable of.

He smiled at them. "Hello, friends. Allow me to introduce myself. I am Gerard, ex-captain of the guard for his majesty, High King Victor Crescent." He bowed with a flourish.

Verika and Elijah exchanged glances. She'd heard, of course, that the high king had been killed, as had the rest of the royal family members. All but one daughter, and apparently she was illegitimate and unable to take the crown.

This reject from drama school must have been involved in that fiasco somehow. "What the hell do you want?" Verika snapped, her nerves fried. Her patience bucket was empty.

He chuckled. "My, my, you must get your manners from your father. Too bad you're not blood-related." He leaned against the wall, looking like an old friend come to visit instead of a murderer.

"Where are they?" she demanded.

"Safe," Gerard said, his eyes shining with malice. "For now."

"If you've done anything to hurt them—" Verika started forward.

"Oh, calm down. I haven't touched them. I've merely

tucked them away where they can't interfere."

"Interfere with what?" Elijah snapped.

Gerard sized him up. Verika knew this was something werewolves tended to do, regardless of whether or not they chose to align themselves with a pack. "I came to offer you a place in our coven," he said, turning his attention to Verika.

She blinked. "What coven?"

"You know," he said, grinning.

What he was asking slowly sank in. "You mean join the Order."

"Precisely."

"Why me? There are thousands of other more powerful witches out there."

"Powerful, yes. Useful, not so much. You have a gift, Verika, for breaking spells. Not everyone possesses such a knack. My mistress has been most interested in you for a while now. Our informant tells us you've come a long way."

It struck her who, exactly, that informant was.

Emilia. Verika swore if she lived through this, the first thing she was doing was going back home and kicking that vindictive witch's pretty little ass.

Verika narrowed her eyes at him. "Well, you can forget it."

"Oh, I wouldn't be so rash to dismiss our invitation." Anger simmered behind his words. "It is a great honor."

"You disgust me! The whole lot of you! Joining you would be the last thing in this world I'd ever do!"

Gerard raised a dark brow. "Even if it meant saving

your parents' lives?"

She stopped.

He smiled. "That's what I thought. At least mull it over. You have twenty-four hours to give me your answer."

"Or what?" Elijah said.

Gerard glanced at him, then at the Mark on Verika's hand. "Then we will come for your mate until we get an answer."

"More like the answer you want," Elijah growled. "She's already told you she's not interested."

"Oh, I think she'll become more interested when her parents are involved. You noble types are so predictable."

"I doubt that," Verika sneered. Raising her hands, she screamed, "Surgent umbrae et serpens!" Shadows shot out of her palms and her eyes turned pitch-black for a moment. The shadows blurred like dark smoke, finally taking on the shape of two snakes with glowing green eyes. They hissed and launched themselves at Gerard.

His eyes widened. "What the—" He darted out of the way about the time the snakes moved to strike. The lights dimmed and the wood floor groaned as shadows seeped from the nooks and crannies, feeding the snakes' size. They grew larger, until they were easily the size of Elijah.

Gerard swore and quickly shifted as the snakes came after him. They tore up the living room in their chase, snapping and hissing and wriggling after their prey. The gray wolf pounced and bounded atop fallen furniture, dancing about the room like a furry ballerina.

At last, Gerard leapt out a window, shattering it. The second the snakes tried to follow outside, the light hit them and they evaporated with pained hisses.

Verika's arms dropped and she sagged to the ground, panting hard.

Elijah fell to his knees beside her. She felt cold all over, as if someone had drenched her in ice water. Her stomach roiled, threatening to erupt again at any minute. God, why was she so sick? It was just a simple conjuring spell. It had never had this effect on her before. But the snakes, the same animal she always conjured, had never been able to feed off darkness like that before either.

Something was wrong. It felt like something that had long since been asleep had awoken inside her. And it wanted out.

"What was that?" Elijah said, gazing at her with a little bit of fear.

"I…" She stared at her hands. The smooth, pale skin of her palm looked so harmless, so normal. No shadows coiled there, like a bed of angry serpents waiting to strike.

Yet, she had seen it, could still feel the dark power writhing deep within her. It was only a pulse, but it was much more pronounced now.

She looked at Elijah, the words lodging in her throat.

"I think… I think that was Black Magic."

CHAPTER EIGHTEEN

VERIKA WAS SHAKING ALL OVER. NOTHING IN HER LIFE
made sense. No matter how long she stared at her
trembling fingers, the shadows didn't manifest again.

Warm, calloused hands took hers. She gripped them
back, needing Elijah's strength right now.

How many times was her life supposed to be flipped
upside-down in one week?

First, there was the revelation that the DPI had been
compromised.

Then she was marked by a werewolf, only to discover
her latent powers of darkness.

"Holy shit," she breathed.

Elijah chuckled.

"It's not funny!" she snapped. She could feel a melt-
down coming on.

"No, no, it's not that. It's just, I could think of several
more colorful expletives to use in a situation like this. You

just discovered you have one of the most desired and rarest forms of magic out there."

"But, I don't know how I got it."

He released her hands and pulled her to the couch. Sitting down was definitely a good idea in this case. Her legs felt like jelly.

"Well, witches can become infected with magic," he suggested.

She appreciated his levelheadedness in this situation. Normally, that was her. But she didn't trust herself to think straight right now. Her whole life had just been derailed.

She nodded. "It's possible. Better than the alternative."

"Would it be terrible having Black Magic?"

She stared at him. "Every Black Witch or Warlock in history has been a murderer. Black Magic is evil."

"I think that might have more to do with the bearer." He reached up and cupped her cheek. "I doubt anyone as good as you could ever be evil. There's a purpose to you having Black Magic. We just have to uncover what it is."

His faith in her was flattering but did little to abate the terror taking over her body.

She swallowed hard. "That man, Gerard... he said he came here for me. It's all my fault my parents are gone."

"Don't you dare say that. Gerard's a prick and you had nothing to do with his actions."

"But we don't know where to find my parents. What if they're already dead and he was just lying?"

"Hey." He lifted her chin with the crook of his finger. "Don't think like that. We're going to find them. I promise."

His promises were so sweet. She wanted to keep

staring into his eyes, to believe in what he said.

But she'd been fed pretty lies before. Life had a way of making you cautious.

He stood, pulling her up with him, and looked around. His eyes narrowed on something by the window. Striding across the room, he knelt, picked up a tuft of fur, and sniffed. His wolf eyes shone gold for a few seconds. "Looks like one of your vipers got a piece of him."

"Can you track him?" she asked, walking to him.

He grinned. "You bet your pretty little ass I can."

"Good," she said, feeling her blood simmer with anger. The darkness inside her stirred at the vengeful thoughts going on inside her head. She'd have to be extra cautious. The history books of her race said darker thoughts often fueled Black Magic because of its fundamental nature. Some had lost control of it altogether by surrendering to their darkest desires.

"You ready for this?" he asked, concern mixed with the eagerness to hunt shining in his eyes.

"Yeah." The shadows in the room darkened. "I think I am."

CHAPTER NINETEEN

Aᴌʟ ᴛʜɪɴɢs ᴀsɪᴅᴇ, ᴛʀᴀᴄᴋɪɴɢ ᴡᴀs ᴏɴᴇ ᴏғ Eʟɪᴊᴀʜ's favorite activities. The ability to follow a trail to its end was something he'd never grown tired of and one of the few aspects of being a werewolf he truly enjoyed.

It didn't take long for them to find Gerard. The viper must have pierced his hide; the smell of blood underscored Gerard's wolfy scent. It fueled the growing rage inside Elijah at another werewolf attacking his mate. Wolves were territorial by nature, and Gerard had just thrown down the gauntlet.

Elijah couldn't wait to reciprocate.

Verika wasn't joking—the town really did die when the sun went down. They followed the scent to an old slaughterhouse on the outskirts of town. The rank smell of death permeated his nostrils as Verika hopped off his back and he shifted back into a human. She handed him the pair of clothes and shoes she'd brought along in her duffel bag, along with a magical arsenal. Gerard was about to get jacked up.

Elijah dressed quickly.

"I don't like this place," Verika said as they slowly entered the building. Blood drops stained the ground near the side entrance, which looked like it had been pried open by claws. The rusting door hadn't stood a chance against a werewolf. The metal was bent and scratched along the rim.

"Kind of reminds you of the set for a horror movie, doesn't it?" he whispered. She smacked him on the arm along with giving him a stern look.

He shrugged. "Sorry. Couldn't resist."

"While I appreciate your efforts at lightening the mood, this is not the time," she said tightly. She'd brought her gun, and raised it, along with a flashlight. Elijah knew from how his nostrils burned that the bullets were made of silver.

Good. Maybe one of them would find its way to Gerard's heart.

They stayed together as they explored the factory. Hooks hung from the ceiling, and large dark splatters stained the floor. It turned his stomach to imagine what went on in here. Sure, he ate meat. He loved the hell out of some chicken. But seeing where the animals were slaughtered made him feel a bit guilty. And sad.

Don't go soft now, he said to himself. *You're a werewolf. You can't forget that.*

After all the horrors he'd seen and the crimes he'd committed, you'd think he'd have a stone heart by now.

Yet, no matter how much pain and suffering he'd endured, he never quite lost his ability to empathize with other animals. He wondered if all werewolves were like that, or if it was just him. Even as a farm boy, he'd seemed to share a bond with the animals his brothers never quite managed.

The winds were restless outside. Judging from the slate-gray hue of the horizon, it looked like a storm was moving in. Thunder echoed in the distance. The old slaughterhouse groaned as the wind beat against it. The first drops of rain fell, heralded by a clap of thunder that rattled Elijah's bones. The storm hit at full strength. It sounded like thousands of pebbles were slamming against the outside of the metal building. The sound was deafening.

Elijah gritted his teeth and tuned it out as they explored the second level. It looked much the same as the first—empty.

Elijah picked up a whiff of something and sniffed harder. Gerard's werewolf scent was stronger up here.

"We're getting closer," he said quietly.

Verika gave a curt nod that she'd heard him. They kept walking. Elijah was ready to throw his body in front of hers if he had to.

They rounded a corner and Verika swiftly turned her flashlight and gun on the open door.

He heard her sharp intake of breath. She rushed forward and fell to her knees beside the two slumped figures of her parents.

"Mom! Dad!" Her eyes were fearful as she took them

in. They didn't respond, though their bellies and chests moved as they breathed.

Elijah's shoulders relaxed some. "They're alive..." He sniffed. "I don't smell any blood."

Verika studied them, growing frustrated. Closing her eyes briefly, she reached into her bag of supplies. "He's bewitched them with some kind of a sleeping spell. I have to break it."

"I wouldn't do that if I were you."

They both whirled toward the doorway. Gerard stood there, donned in nothing but a dark cloak. He looked significantly more ruffled than he had earlier at the house.

Elijah instantly leapt in front of Verika, growling.

Gerard grinned, his own eyes flashing gold. "What a charming guard dog. I can see why my mistress coveted you so."

A sliver of fear wriggled its way through Elijah's bloodstream, leaving ice in its wake.

"However, I have no use for you," Gerard said, waving his hand dismissively at Elijah. He gazed at Verika hungrily. "What I'm really interested in is how you came to possess the power of darkness and death."

Verika stood, and positioned herself in front of her parents. "I don't know."

"Oh, but it seems your mentor did."

Verika blinked. "What are you talking about?" she asked in a small voice.

Gerard held up a small leather-bound journal. "After our little encounter, I returned here to burrow through some of the journals I'd apprehended from Satine. She was quite the collector of odd spells. But none of her spells were quite so odd as the one used to bind your powers when you were a baby."

"How do you know this?" Verika whispered.

"It's all right here," Gerard insisted, tapping the volume. "As written by your mother. She documented *everything* about you and your past."

Verika's heart skipped a beat as she stared at it.

"Yes," Gerard purred. "You want it, don't you?" When Verika didn't answer, Gerard added, "Don't you want to know where you came from? Who your true parents were? Don't you want to know the truth?"

Verika's hands trembled as she curled her fingers into fists. "Yes," she said quietly, hiding her gaze. "I want to know all those things and more." She raised her defiant eyes to his. "But that's still not enough of a lure to get me to submit to your Order."

He went stone-still. "Are you sure you won't reconsider?"

"Positive," Verika said, without hesitation.

Elijah braced himself as Gerard's eyes flashed gold. "Very well. My mistress will not suffer a fool."

"Neither will I," Verika said. Elijah—and evidently Gerard—hadn't noticed she'd slipped her hand inside her bag while they'd been talking. She flung a vial of ink at him, muttering something in Latin.

The vial shot forward with blue and purple sparks, slamming into an astonished Gerard's face. He hissed and cursed as the ink coated his eyes. He stumbled backward, swiping at his face with the hem of his cloak.

Elijah seized the moment. He charged forward, shifting as his feet thundered against the ground. His paws connected with Gerard's shoulders, causing Gerard to stagger backwards toward the railed walkway. The two of them tumbled over the ledge, plummeting to the cement floor below.

Verika screamed his name, and he saw her rush forward to grip the railing. He barked at her once, hoping she'd catch the hint to get her parents and scram. He leapt off Gerard as the man shifted violently and righted himself so he landed on his paws at the last second.

A bloody battle ensued. The gray and black wolves lunged and snarled at each other as the storm raged on outside. Nails and teeth shone in the lightning flashes, and freshly spilled blood glistened along the floor.

Gerard had learned to fight dirty. Elijah could tell that much. Every ounce of his concentration was centered on keeping the gray wolf from taking a bite out of his neck. He had to keep his mate safe, whatever the cost.

That's probably why he didn't notice that the shadows seemed to be growing darker. They spread from the corners of the slaughterhouse and along the floor like ink. The edge of the pool of darkness writhed with claws, as if it were searching for something.

Or someone.

The second it touched Gerard, an oily hand shot out of the darkness. It latched onto Gerard's back leg midlunge, jerking him backward. The wolf gave a yelp as he hit the floor, digging his claws in as the shadows pulled him backwards, toward the ever-expanding pool.

Elijah backed away. The shadows seemed uninterested in him, and thank God for that. What he saw... it was unnatural, as if the darkness had taken on a life of its own. He swore he heard moaning and the gnashing of teeth as the gray wolf whined and barked in his struggle to break free. He didn't cry out in pain until his back legs began to sink slowly into the goop.

Elijah trembled as the darkness literally devoured him. Bit by bit, the majestic gray wolf was eaten alive by the ink, until there was nothing but the head left. By then, Gerard had shifted back to a human.

His terrified eyes landed on something behind Elijah. Gulping, he turned.

There stood his mate, wreathed in shadows and a murky green glow. Her eyes shone green, and her hair whipped and coiled about her head like angry serpents. A single arm was outstretched, her fist slowly closing. The shadows responded, pulling Gerard further in as she formed a fist.

"Please," Gerard whispered, his voice filled with pain. "Have mercy."

When Verika spoke, her voice wasn't her own. It was powerful and devoid of any emotion. It scared the hell out of Elijah. *It's the Black Magic talking.*

"You didn't show Satine mercy," she said.

Gerard rasped a laugh. "So, you're doing this for revenge. There may be hope for you after all."

"I'll never be like you."

"Not now, maybe, but in time." He grinned. It was the smile of a lunatic. "You could have a great deal to

141

learn from my mistress."

Elijah shifted back and glared at Gerard. "Forget it. Neither my mate nor I are ever getting tangled up with that woman again."

Gerard's cackle echoed off the barren, metallic walls. "Do you think you're free from her? You're never free from her."

"I will be once she's dead."

Gerard wheezed a laugh. "Then it won't matter at that time, because you, too, will be dead."

"What the hell are you talking about?"

"Didn't you know? Those markings on you... they weren't just to swear allegiance to the Order. They were created through Blood Magic, using *her blood*, and thus, can only be undone by her blood. The two of you are soul-bound. If she dies, you die."

Verika gasped. Her magic faltered, and Gerard started to climb out of the tar pit.

Elijah whirled. "Don't listen to him! He's just trying to distract you!"

"You wish!" Gerard yelled, trying to pull himself out. "It's the truth! I dare you to see otherwise."

Elijah stilled. If that was indeed true, then how on earth were he and Verika ever going to be together? They'd never truly be free of Mistress Black.

"Enough of your lies!" Verika spat.

She closed her fist.

With a startled cry, the ink began sucking Gerard in. Elijah realized she'd been holding back.

To savor the moment.

Sure, he'd sought revenge on people before and had drawn it out. But those dark emotions didn't belong in his mate. She was inherently good—he could feel it deep in his soul.

He'd contemplate her dark change of heart later.

"Don't say I didn't warn you!" Gerard yelled, right before he was sucked into the abyss. Verika released the spell with a cry and fell to her knees. The ink quickly retreated to the natural corners where shadows clung.

Elijah went to her, cuddling her against his chest. "Your parents—"

"Are fine," she said, breathing hard. "I found the spell loophole. It will wear off in an hour or so. We'll have them home by then."

He nodded. "Where did you send Gerard?" he asked, casting the shadows an anxious glance.

She gulped, trembling. "Someplace I'd rather not think about."

Fair enough. He helped her to her feet. The two of them held on to each other a moment, lost in their thoughts.

"Was what he said true?" she asked. "Are you really bound to Mistress Black?"

Elijah had to search for an answer. "I want to say no... but I have a feeling in my gut the answer is yes. Mostly because things never turn out well for me. I never get the happily-ever-after ending. I get the let's-make-your-life-hell ending."

Verika's eyes flashed with that menacing green light he'd seen earlier. "Not if I have anything to say about it."

Oh, he hoped she would find it, because if she couldn't figure out how to break the brand, no one could.

Which meant he was in some really deep shit.

CHAPTER TWENTY

Mistress Black felt Gerard's soul leave his body and come barreling into her slumbering body. She bolted upright, gasping. It felt like someone had dumped gasoline on her insides and tossed a lit match onto her.

In other words, it hurt like hell, but she wouldn't scream. There was no room for weakness in the Order, especially from her. She almost welcomed the agony because it made her feel something.

Oh, what it must feel like to be truly alive.

Since getting struck with the curse that had rendered her real body no more than an empty shell, she had been absorbing souls with any magical prowess with the hopes of restoring her own magical abilities so that she may return to her true form. There had been just enough magic left in her dying breath to reach out to a young, impressionable witch and convince her to give up her body so her soul could inhabit it. If she could keep her soul alive, she could restore her body. It had taken time; the witch who'd sealed her powers had been one tough bitch.

Mistress Black looked at her borrowed body in the mirror across from her bed and smirked. As if death would be the end of her. Over the millennia, she had swallowed so many souls, using this body as a conduit to her real one. The old curse was starting to crack. She could feel it; as her powers expanded, it pressed against the confines of the ancient spell.

Soon, she would be herself again. Soon, her darkness would shadow the world and they would regret ever persecuting her kind.

There was much to fear in a Black Witch. Power over death terrified people, and rightly so. But burning her husband and eldest daughter at the stake in front of her house…

People's fears often devolved into cruelty. Watching her family burn had broken something inside of her.

The villagers of her medieval village had awoken a nightmare, and her wrath knew no bounds. She swore over their cold corpses that no other witch or warlock would ever be persecuted that way again. Sacrifices had been made along the way. The quickest way to restore her powers was to absorb the most magical beings of all, namely other witches. It had pained her to use her kind in so crude a way, but she had no other choice.

She had no other choice…

She shook her head. Now was not the time for doubt, not when she was so close to her goal.

Leaning back against the blood-red silk pillows, she turned over and stared at the painting on her nightstand of a little girl with red curls.

Tears shone in her eyes. Though the villagers had claimed her eldest daughter, she had managed to escape with her youngest. She had been a baby at the time. They'd moved from town to town, trying to keep a low profile, but her brilliant red hair had given their identities away. Sacrificing herself to save her daughter's life had been the best thing she'd ever done.

She'd always wondered what kind of a woman she'd grown up into, if she'd found happiness.

Had she found someone to love her? Did they love her as much as her mother did?

She reached out and gently touched the painting. It could never do the real thing justice, but it kept her close.

After one last lingering glance, she'd turned over and closed her eyes when a familiar tingling went through her. She bolted upright, every sense wired.

It couldn't be. That signature hadn't called out to her in centuries, and yet…

Her gaze drifted to the portrait of her daughter.

Idrina.

Those green eyes, the same emerald shade as her own, shone, as if containing a valuable secret.

Throwing back the covers, Mistress Black donned her slippers and silk robe and went to her scrying room, feeling hope for the first time in ages.

There was much explaining to be done after the fight.

Elijah and Verika had ultimately decided to alter her parents' memories of the fight. Instead of being kidnapped and held hostage by a supernatural psychopath, they thought they'd spent a quiet evening at home. Verika felt guilty for doing it, but she didn't want them to be mentally scarred for life. They might not ever trust paranormals again, and thus might not allow her back into their home.

And she needed her family. They were the one thing she couldn't live without.

Well, except the werewolf standing in front of her.

After bespelling her parents so they wouldn't remember ever seeing them, Verika bid them farewell, with a knot in her throat the size of Texas. She hated manipulating people's minds, but it was for their own good. No way was she going to risk getting the people she loved hurt again. She was too dangerous to be around.

It's better this way. Really, it is, she told herself, as she and Elijah left. Still, it didn't make what she'd done any easier a pill to swallow.

Elijah said nothing, only grabbing her hand and squeezing it. Understanding shone in his eyes.

He knew better than anyone what she was giving up. It had been ages since he'd seen his brothers. No matter how much he wanted to reconnect, he knew, ultimately, he couldn't. For the sake of their well-being, he had to stay away.

She smiled at him. At least they had each other, two outcasts who never quite fit in anywhere else, except in each other's arms.

They stopped by a gas station to get cheap food and a pay-by-minute phone. Then Elijah shifted, and together they ran into the woods.

Elijah ran most of the way. Even with Verika cloaking their whereabouts, they couldn't take any chances on letting the DPI catch up to them. If her coworker had been part of the Order, there was no telling who else had been compromised. Staying behind was too great a risk.

It was nearly dusk by the time they stopped. They built a fire to keep away the evening chill, which Verika cloaked to make it invisible to everyone. She then set the area with an assortment of alarm and repulsion spells. This way, if someone stumbled upon them, they would feel an intense urge to leave, though they wouldn't know why.

They ate their gas station food and drank water as they sat by the fire. The flames chased away the chill, but Verika still felt cold inside.

She was a Black Witch, the rarest gift of magic.

"You okay?"

She looked up to find Elijah watching her.

"Yeah." She sighed. "It's just a lot to take in."

"You can handle it. You wouldn't have gotten a gift that powerful if you couldn't. And I can't think of a better witch to have inherited so strong a gift."

"What if it's a curse?" she whispered.

He stared at her thoughtfully. "I think it's what you make of it. If you dread your powers, they probably will be a curse. If you embrace them, they'll be less of a burden. You may even come to enjoy them."

She thought about that. Could she embrace being a

Black Witch? Could she learn to overcome her fear of herself and even cherish it?

She had a long way to go before that happened. And before it could…

She glanced at the Mark, then at the sky. A few stars poked out of the darkening blue expanse. What really stood out was the large white orb. "It's a full moon."

He went still, looking away. "Yeah."

"It's the last night for us to, um, mate."

"Yeah," he said, quieter.

They sat in silence for a minute.

"You don't have to—"

"Elijah—" They stopped and chuckled.

Verika took a deep breath to steady her nerves. Slowly, she lifted her eyes to him. "I want to."

Elijah's head jerked up. He went still. "You do?"

She nodded.

He stared at her for a moment longer. Then he grabbed her wrist and pulled her to him. His mouth came down on hers with such fervor she barely had time to register what was happening. God, she could get used to being kissed like this.

She was drowning in him, could feel herself growing wetter for him. A moan slipped from her mouth as he tipped her head back and kissed her neck. "Are you sure?" he breathed against her slightly sweat-dampened skin.

She found his eyes and smiled. "I've never been so sure about anything." She blinked, confused. "But I thought we needed a pack to, um, 'witness' the occasion."

"Not with a rogue, you don't, since I don't officially

have a pack. I'm a lone wolf." He cupped her face and kissed her forehead. "Besides, you're my pack now."

She slowly smiled at him as her eyes teared up.

His eyes softened. His kisses were different as he laid her back against the soft grass and began undressing her. His lips moved in tender gestures as clothing came off, and skin came into contact with skin.

She sighed with contentment as he kissed a path straight from her jawline to her aching breasts. Her nipples were pert; he took each of them into his mouth, one and then the other, sucking and gently nipping. She moaned and arched her back, feeling her toes curl as he cupped and squeezed her breasts.

The fire inside of her, the need to mate with him, was growing stronger.

His mouth at last traveled back up to hers, planting another breathless kiss there. She gazed up at him in wonder. How had she been so fortunate to end up with this magnificent creature? His muscles were bathed in moonlight, and his eyes faintly glowed gold. He looked like an elven king, come to claim her in his domain.

She could feel his swollen cock prodding her wet opening, seeking entrance. She instinctively opened her legs a little wider.

"Are you ready?" he asked, his voice ragged.

She closed her eyes and kissed him in response, without even taking another breath.

That was all the invitation he needed. He thrust. She gasped as he entered her and began pumping, slowly pushing his considerable girth inside of her. Slowly, she loosened up, her nectar coating his cock and easily allowing him to immerse himself fully.

He groaned as he finally thrust himself all the way inside. God, he was so big. He filled her up completely, and yet, it didn't hurt. She felt... whole, like a piece of her that had been missing was finally rejoined.

She whimpered and clung to him as he began slowly rocking inside her. He didn't pull all the way out, for which she was glad. Considering his size, it probably would have hurt. No, he was a gentle lover.

He kissed her tenderly as he made love to her, each thrust of his powerful hips carefully controlled so as not to hurt her. He was so sweet. She eagerly brought her hips up to meet him as he pumped, the embers of pleasure inside of her threatening to turn into an inferno at any second.

The sensations spilled over her body in one powerful burst, and she cried out.

He kissed her cheek, still pumping. "Are you okay?" he breathed.

"Yes," she whispered back, her voice ragged. She laughed a little and hugged him, placing her mouth beside his ear. "Why don't you roll over onto your back so I can help you?"

His rhythm stumbled a bit as his brow arched. He stared at her and then blinked before complying. "Yes, ma'am."

In an instant, he'd grabbed her and swung them so he was on his back. She yelped and giggled, then sighed at the feeling of straddling him. It was a totally new sensation, but a damned good one.

Sitting straight up, she began riding him, sliding herself over his shaft in desperate movements. He groaned, holding onto her hips and squeezing. She reached down and grabbed his hands, guiding them to her bouncing breasts.

He eagerly complied and began playing with them. He held onto them, squeezing and kneading and teasing her nipples with his forefingers and thumbs.

She tossed her head back, breathing in the crisp night air and feeling freer than she had in a long time.

He let her work him, which she was definitely enjoying. A deep groan that was almost a growl came up his throat, right before she felt his hot seed pour into her. He groaned again, thrusting his hips a few times before lying still at last, panting.

She was breathing much harder herself. Climbing off him, she curled up beside him.

He was right—the mating had worked. Their tattoos were complete. She admired the elegant indigo swirls crisscrossing on their chests, shoulders, and backs. The pattern shimmered in the moonlight, as if they were made from stardust. She'd been so caught up in the intense pleasure of the moment that she'd barely registered the slight tingling sensation across her skin as the tattoo spread.

Intense happiness swelled in her chest, and she found herself almost in tears again. For a long while, neither of them spoke, content to let the enormity of what they'd just shared sink in.

They stared at the growing number of stars dotting the darkening sky. "Have you looked at the journal yet?"

Elijah asked softly.

Verika shook her head, cuddling closer to him. "No. I'm not… *ready*. Satine, my mother… they must have had a good reason to bind my powers. It's because they're evil."

"What if it was because she didn't want you to be overwhelmed by them? I still think it's the witch who makes the magic, not the other way around."

Verika was silent as she thought. She wanted so desperately to believe her mate. Could she learn to control her powers? Would she ever not fear them?

"Being afraid of yourself sucks," she grumbled against his chest.

He chuckled, the deep sound rumbling through her. "I know the feeling."

She swallowed hard, her thoughts switching topics. "Are you ready to see your brothers?"

Elijah grew silent. "Yes," he finally said. His voice was a fearful whisper, so full of hope, yet so weighed down by the fear of disappointment. He took a deep breath and let it out in one long gush. "What if they don't want to hear what I have to say, about why I've been absent for so long without any contact?"

"I'm sure they'll be a little mad," she admitted calmly. "But I'm also sure they still love you and want you back in their lives. They'd rather face Mistress Black with you than abandon you. Sure, you've made mistakes, but so have they. We all have."

He squeezed her shoulders in a brief hug and sat up. He ran his hands over his face and through his hair. "What should I do? I don't have a clue how to go about this."

Verika sat up and dug through her bag. Smiling, she held up her pay-by-minute phone.

"How about we start with letting them know you're alive?"

The conversation with Gage was stilted, as Verika had expected it to be. How on earth did you tell someone their brother, whom they believed to be dead, was alive and sitting right in front of you? Not to mention he'd sounded annoyed when he'd first barked into the phone.

"Well?" Elijah said, waiting nearby. He looked tense.

Her lips spread into a grin. "It's a start. Now let's go find your brothers."

END OF BOOK 4

SACRIFICE

BLOOD MOON RISING #5

LOLA TAYLOR

Read about Nik, Alara, and all your favorite werewolves in *Sacrifice*, now available.

OTHER BOOKS BY
LOLA TAYLOR

The Her Dark Desires Trilogy
Carnal (free for a limited time!)
Sinful
Soulful (coming soon!)

Blood Moon Rising
Fever (free for a limited time!)
Protector
Betrayal
Captured
Sacrifice
Ritual

Blood Moon Rising companion novels
Lust
Forever (coming soon!)

Standalone novels
Shatter

For a full list of titles, please visit
www.lolataylorbooks.com.

For more information, please visit
www.lolataylorbooks.com

Your opinion matters—please leave a review!

Thank you for reading my book! If you have a moment, I'd really appreciate an honest rating and review. They help authors stand out in a busy marketplace, plus they give browsing readers the nitty-gritty on books they're shopping. Everyone wins when you rate and review, so please do! Your opinion counts!

ABOUT THE AUTHOR

"Lola Taylor" is a pen name created for the romances I can't show my grandma without blushing. My favorite genre to write is romantic suspense, usually involving hot werewolves, warlocks, or any other type of paranormal creature. Keep the action hot and the romance hotter—that's my motto! I'm a horror film junkie, I still love Halloween as an adult (seriously, I think I get more excited for it than some kids do), and what precious spare time I have is spent with my family, reading (everything from sci fi to middle grade), playing the flute, painting pretty pictures, or screwing around on Pinterest or Etsy. Hailing from the South, I currently live in the Midwest with five fur babies and my hubby.

You can connect with me on Facebook (www.facebook.com/lolataylorbooks) or my email (lolawritespnr@gmail.com). Learn more about me and my books at www.lolataylorbooks.com.